Pra
Ghost Stories and

'Spooky stories, sp(
recommend it.'
Della Galton, short story writer, novelist and writing teacher

'A great mix of stories and commentary which between them will give you all the tools you need to give it a go yourself. Written in a chatty, no-nonsense style.'
Helen Hunt, short story writer, writing teacher
and Writers' Forum columnist

Praise for
Short Stories and How to Write Them

'A delightful collection of short stories…a generous selection of tips on improving your writing…ideal for writers of all abilities.'
Morgen Bailey, novelist, short story writer,
blogger, editor and writing teacher

'If you write – or would like to write – fiction for women's magazines, this is THE Kindle download for you.'
Sally Zigmond, novelist and prize-winning short story writer

ISBN-13: 978-1495485220
ISBN-10: 1495485226

This edition published 2014

This book is also available as an ebook.

Please visit www.kathleenmcgurl.com
for more information and for contact details

Cover image from www.dreamstime.com
Cover design by Connor McGurl
and Chris Callow

Kathleen McGurl

Ghost Stories

and

How to Write Them

An anthology of women's magazine ghost stories
plus notes on how to write your own

Also by Kathleen McGurl

Short Stories

and

How to Write Them

*An anthology of women's magazine stories
plus notes on how to write your own*

CONTENTS

Introduction

About this book

Hello, and thanks for reading my book! Before we start, I'd like to share a few words about what's in this book, as it doesn't quite fall into any regular genre. Is it an anthology, or a How to Write book? Well, it's both. It contains a collection of my ghost stories, most of which have previously been published in women's magazines in the UK. But it also contains my musings on what makes a good ghost story for this market, and hints and tips on how to write one yourself.

I went through a phase some years back of writing almost nothing but ghost stories, and I thought a lot about what made them work. I'm happy to say I sold most of them, so I must have got something right. Now, I thought I'd write up all those ideas, using my own published stories as examples. I hope you like the resulting book.

If you've bought it because you like reading ghost stories and aren't interested in writing them, feel free to skip through the discussion sections and go straight to the stories. If you are more interested in learning how to write ghost stories for women's magazines, feel free to skip the stories, though they do illustrate the points I want to make. Personally I'd prefer you to start at the beginning and read through to the end but hey, it's your copy of the book, you read it however you like! As long as you enjoy it.

From now on, rather than write 'women's magazines' over and over, I'm going to use the term 'womag' for short. Some readers will already know me as 'womagwriter', via my blog *womagwriter.blogspot.co.uk* which is themed around writing short stories for women's magazines, and contains advice and guidelines for writers. There's a post somewhere on my blog about writing ghost stories. This book is really an enormous expansion of that post.

What is a short story?

We'd better start at the beginning, and determine what is a short story, before discussing what is a womag ghost story. I'll only cover this part briefly, and suggest that you read Della Galton's wonderful book, *How to Write and Sell Short Stories*, for more detail.

A short story has a beginning, a middle and an end. A successful womag story will start with a character who has a problem (the beginning). During the course of the story, the character needs to resolve the problem, through her own actions. It won't be straightforward and things may get worse (the middle) before they get better and the issue is resolved (the end). By the way, I say 'her' actions, but you can have male main characters as well. Having said that, most published stories tend to involve female main characters. From now on I will refer to 'main character' as 'MC'.

So, your MC starts with a problem, which she resolves, so that by the end of the story she is in a better situation than she was at the beginning. Womag stories DO need to have happy, hopeful or uplifting endings.

Now then, because I've recently read Scarlett Thomas's book, *Monkeys with Typewriters*, (isn't that a great title?) in which she explains story structure, I'm going to pass on a little of my newly acquired knowledge to you, and go on for a bit about Ancient Greeks.

Aristotle identified three main types of story – the Epic, the Tragedy and the Comedy.

We all know what an Epic is – a long tale with various ups and downs; usually the characters are going on some sort of quest. Think *Lord of the Rings*. Womag stories are never Epics.

For the difference between Tragedies and Comedies, we're going to have to get a bit mathematical. Before your eyes glaze over, it is very simple, honest! I found it incredibly useful to start thinking of story structure in this way. In a Tragedy, the MC starts out pretty well off, all things considered. Rich, powerful, happy, she's already got what she wants. In the early part of the story, things get better still for this character. But pride comes before a fall, and when things start to go bad they go *really* bad, ending with the MC hitting rock bottom and dying. Either literally (in Shakespeare's historical tragedies) or metaphorically. Here's the maths bit – we can draw a graph of the story arc:

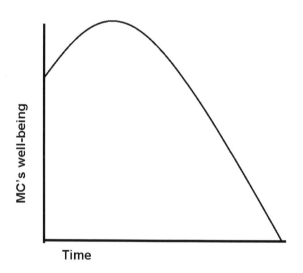

Tragedy Story Arc

I hope you can see that womag stories are never tragedies, either. Earlier I said that in a womag story the MC ends up in a better place than she started from. And *that* is the story arc of a comedy. I don't mean (and neither did Aristotle) comedy as in ha-ha, split your sides laughing. It's comedy as in a tale with a happy ending. So let's do the maths bit and look at a graph showing the comedy story arc:

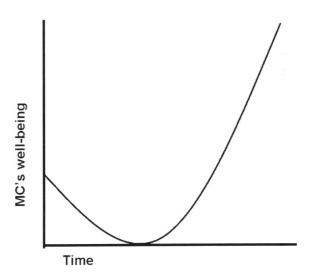

Comedy Story Arc

That's more like it! At the start of the story the MC is low down on the well-being axis — because she has a problem. Things get worse before they get better, but she eventually ends up in a much better state.

Womag stories are *always* comedies, in this sense of the word. Study some, and you'll see this!

Finally, to finish this section, I must unreservedly apologise to anyone who has studied the classics, for what is probably a very poor summary of Aristotle's *Poetics* (which I admit I have never read. I am paraphrasing Scarlett Thomas here.) But this is how I understand it, and thinking about story arc can really help you to structure your writing.

What is a womag ghost story?

This book's supposed to be all about ghost stories, so it is about time I started talking about them. The first thing to bear in mind is that womag ghost stories are gentle things. They're not scary. There's no blood and gore in them. They won't keep you awake at night after reading them, wondering what's under the bed and why there's a strange tapping noise coming from the wardrobe (it'll be your pipes). They might send a little shiver down your spine, maybe at the low point of the story arc (womag ghost stories follow the comedy story arc, of course!) but they'll end happily and it is perfectly safe to read them on your own, late at night. Unless you are *particularly* sensitive.

So what IS a womag ghost story? I think there are three main types. At least most of mine fall into these three types. If you read or write a lot of ghost stories you might come up with different ideas, but this is my classification, and there are several examples of each of these types in this book:

1. Stories in which the *ghost* is the character with the problem, which must be resolved before the ghost can truly rest in peace.

2. Stories in which the ghostly presence helps the MC come to terms with a loss, usually the loss of who ever the ghost was when it was alive.

3. Stories where something spooky happens, but there is an alternative rational explanation, to appeal to people who don't or won't believe in the supernatural.

OK, that's enough theory for now. It's time we had our first story. I'm going to kick off with one of my favourites. It's a Type 1 story – a ghost with a problem. But as you'll see, the ghost's problem causes difficulties for the living characters as well. This story was originally published in *Take A Break's Fiction Feast* in 2008.

We'll Meet Again

Kelly was wearing a new brooch. A large amber, surrounded by marcasite, set in gold-coloured metal. Nice, but rather old-fashioned for a seventeen-year old, I thought.

'That's pretty, love,' I told her.

'Got it off eBay,' she said, fingering it proudly. 'It's 1930s. I like this old stuff.'

Kelly had recently discovered eBay. She'd sold her old Barbie dolls on the online auction site, and then she'd bid for some DVDs which she'd got for a fraction of the shop price. Now she'd begun looking at costume jewellery and clothes. It was a good way for her to spend some of the money she earned from her Saturday job.

But lately, everything she bought was vintage – from the 1930s or 1940s. I supposed she was trying to forge a new style for herself. Girls of that age like to be different from the crowd.

'It's just a phase,' Mike said, when I talked to him about it. 'And rather vintage than punk, I say.'

Her next purchase was a 1940s tea dress. It was made of flowered cotton, had a Peter Pan collar and mother-of-pearl buttons.

Lovely – in a museum-piece kind of way. I wondered if she was turning into a collector, but she began wearing the dress around the house, changing into it as soon as she got home from college.

'It feels right, Mum,' she said. 'Like it goes with the house.'

We'd moved into the house about a month before. It was pre-war, and packed with original features. We'd inherited it from my spinster great-aunt Betty, who'd lived here all her life. My grandmother, now 90 and in a retirement home, hadn't wanted us to move in.

'There's something strange about that house, you know,' she'd warned. 'There are things you don't know about. Things that happened a long time ago. You want to be careful, in that house. There's a *presence* there.'

'Don't be silly, Gran,' I'd said. 'You grew up there. It can't be that bad. And I don't believe in ghosts.' But Gran had pursed her lips and refused to say anything more.

Over the next few weeks, Kelly acquired more vintage clothes, and began wearing them all the time.

'I like them, Mum,' she said. 'In any case, that's all I can find on eBay these days.'

'What do you mean?' I said. 'There's loads of contemporary stuff.'

'Not for me,' Kelly replied. 'Come on, I'll show you.'

She went to the computer and opened up eBay. I watched her set up a search for women's clothing. A page appeared showing thumbnail photos of items, with brief descriptions alongside.

'There you are, you see,' I said. 'Those all modern things. Look at that lovely leather jacket! And that gorgeous dress from Monsoon!'

Kelly just looked sideways at me, then clicked on the Monsoon dress. But the page which opened up showed something completely different – a plain, pale yellow blouse with a rounded collar and set-in sleeves. *Genuine 1940s blouse,* said the details. *Some repairs to hem, but otherwise perfect condition.*

'Hmm, I like that one,' Kelly said, dreamily. 'It would go with my navy skirt.'

'Love, you haven't got a navy skirt,' I said. Kelly shook her head and looked at me, her big brown eyes filled with worry.

'I know I haven't, Mum. But *she* has.'

'Who's she?' I asked, but Kelly stood up and went to her bedroom without replying. I sat down at the computer and clicked the Refresh button. The yellow blouse disappeared, and in its place was a photo of the Monsoon dress.

'Kelly,' I called. 'Come and look at this – I'll pay for it if you'd like it.' I wanted my twenty-first century girl back again – jeans and all.

Kelly came back downstairs wearing one of her forties' frocks. She'd pulled her hair back into a thick hairnet at the nape of her neck. 'Mum, call me Joan, please, from now on. I hate the name Kelly.'

The next day she refused to go to college. 'It seems so indulgent, Mother. Wasting my time studying literature when all those poor souls are suffering. I want to do something more important with my time.'

'Like what, Kelly?'

'Joan. I asked you to call me Joan. I don't know. Maybe I can get a job driving ambulances. Or in the munitions factory.'

She spent the day knitting socks. When Mike came home we had a whispered conversation in the hallway.

'I'm worried, Mike. This isn't just a phase. It's more like – I don't know – like she's possessed.'

'Possessed – that's a strong word, Ali. By whom?'

'Joan, whoever she is. Or was.'

'Did someone call my name?' Kelly said, coming out of the living room. 'Oh hello, Father. I'm glad you're home safe, and before the blackout begins.'

'Blackout?' said Mike. 'Father? I'm your *Dad,* Kelly. And this nonsense has to stop. Wearing all these ancient clothes and acting as though there's a war on. It's 2014, for goodness sake! And you'd better not miss any more days at college, or you'll never pass those exams.'

Kelly just stood, head bowed, hands clasped in front of her while he spoke. When he finished, she nodded meekly. 'Yes, Father.'

At the weekend, Kelly asked if she could move her things into the spare room. 'This was always my room, Mother. It's full of happy memories for me.'

'We've only lived here two months, love,' I said.

'But I've always been here,' she replied. 'I was born here. So were my sisters, Margaret and Betty.'

I felt a cold shiver run down my spine. Margaret was my grandmother. Betty was my great-aunt who'd left us the house. But they hadn't had a third sister – that I knew of. My grandmother's words came back to me – *there are things you don't know. Things that happened. A presence, in the house.*

I resolved to ask Gran about Joan. Maybe I'd take Kelly with me.

'That's a pretty dress, dear,' Gran said, when we arrived at her home. 'My sister used to have one just like it.' Kelly was wearing her 1940s flowered tea dress.

'Your sister, Betty?' I asked.

'No, er, yes. That's right. My sister Betty.'

Normally I'd assumed Gran's uncertainty was down to her age, but now I wasn't sure. Was she hiding something?

'Gran,' I asked. 'Who was Joan?'

'Where did you hear that name?' she snapped.

Kelly stared at her. 'It's my name, now.'

'It's not your name. Though you are very like her, especially in that dress,' Gran said.

'Like who, Gran?'

'Her. Joan.' She sighed. 'I suppose it won't hurt to say, now Betty's gone. Joan was our other sister. She died, during the war.'

'Oh Gran, how sad! Why did you never talk about her?'

'Betty didn't want me to. Joan killed herself, you see. She was only seventeen. My parents and Betty were ashamed – there was a stigma attached to suicide in those days, you know.'

'The poor girl,' I said, glancing at Kelly. She was white. 'Why… why was she so unhappy?'

'She'd had a sweetheart. His name was – '

'Jack McBride,' finished Kelly. Gran and I turned to look at her, open-mouthed.

'How did you know that?' Gran asked.

'He was tall, dark haired and dimpled,' Kelly said, staring at the wall, focussed on something only she could see. 'We were going to marry.'

Gran spoke quietly, watching Kelly. 'Joan had promised to marry him, on his next leave. And our parents had given their consent. But poor Jack – '

'– never made it back. He was killed on the Normandy beaches, on D-Day. Deliverance Day!' spat Kelly. 'Death Day, more like.'

'She's right,' whispered Gran. 'And Joanie was so angry. Just like Kelly is now. It's as though – as though Joanie's come back to us, in Kelly.'

'I have come back, Margaret,' said Kelly, taking Gran's hands in hers. 'I'm here.'

'But,' I gasped, 'where's Kelly? Where's my daughter?'

'She's here,' Kelly, or Joan, said. 'We're, well, sharing her body, I suppose.'

'But Joanie,' Gran said. 'Kelly's young, she has her life ahead of her. Leave her be!'

'I had my life ahead of me too,' said Joan, bitterly. 'Till Churchill sent my Jack to die on the beaches. I killed myself to be with him. But I can't find him, Margaret. I can't find him!' She buried her face in her hands and sobbed. My heart went out to her. Kelly hadn't cried like that since she was a little girl. And no seventeen-year old in love should have to lose her fiancé like that.

'Joan,' I said. It felt so strange to call my daughter by that name. 'Is that what you want? To find Jack, again?'

She looked up at me, her eyes ringed black with tear-stained mascara. 'Yes,' she said. 'That's all I want.'

I'd had an idea.

Mike thought it just might work. 'We have to resolve this somehow, Ali,' he said. 'We want our vibrant young Kelly back. And a holiday in France isn't a bad idea, in any case.'

A few days later we took the car ferry to Le Havre. I'd spent a few hours on Kelly's beloved computer, which she hadn't touched since Joan had taken over, researching the D-Day landings. I'd found out where Jack's company had been sent, and where the casualties had been buried. Finally I'd struck lucky, and the Commonwealth War Graves Commission website had given me the information I needed.

It was about an hour's drive from Le Havre to Banneville-la-Campagne. The cemetery was just 100 metres from the main road. We parked the car, then Mike twisted round to speak to Joan.

'Now, do you know why we're here?'

She nodded, slowly. She'd been quiet for the whole journey. I wasn't sure if she was looking forward to finding Jack, or dreading it. Perhaps she didn't know herself.

'Come on, then,' Mike said, and we all got out of the car. I helped Gran out, and handed her a walking stick. She'd insisted on coming with us.

'She's my little sister, Alison. This might be difficult for her, and I want to be there for her.'

We made our way slowly past the rows of white crosses, each one marking a story as tragic as Jack's. And for each Jack, there could be a Joan. All those wasted and ruined lives. I silently prayed for them as I passed each grave.

And there he was. Plot D673. A white cross, like all the others, surrounded by neatly tended lawn. The only difference between this and the thousands of others was the name inscribed into the stone. Captain Jack McBride, June 6th, 1944.

Joan gasped. 'Jack, oh my Jack!'

Gran caught hold of her arm. 'His body's here, Joan. Is he here, for you?'

Joan turned to her sister with shining eyes. 'He's here, Margaret. And he's waited for me! I've found him, after all these years!'

The two sisters hugged each other – one frail and old, the other a teenager. 'Goodbye, Joanie,' said Gran. 'Go to him, now.'

'Goodbye, Mags. And thank you,' she said, turning to Mike and me. It was an awkward moment. Did we say goodbye too, to our *daughter?*

While we hesitated, a faint mist rose up from Jack's grave. For a moment I thought I saw the outline of a tall man, in uniform. The mist drifted towards Joan, enveloped her, then dispersed, as quickly as it had formed.

Kelly shook her head and blinked. 'Mum, I really hope you've brought some decent clothes for me to change into. I am *so* sick of these blinking dowdy frocks.'

'Kelly! You're back!' Mike and I both rushed to hug her.

Gran was crying quietly into her handkerchief. 'Good to have you back, young Kelly,' she said, kissing her great-granddaughter's cheek.

'Of course I've brought some clothes, love!' I said. 'Come on, they're in the car.' I'd secretly packed jeans, a t-shirt and her favourite Ugg boots she'd found on eBay before Joan took over. Mike and I linked arms with her, and we walked, laughing and chatting, towards the car park.

I glanced back, to see Gran still standing for a moment longer at the grave. We'd regained a daughter, but she'd lost a sister, for the second time. When the time came, I'd bring her ashes here, to scatter where she'd be able to find her sister once more.

The End

We'll Meet Again – Discussion

I told this story from Ali's point of view, and Ali's problem is that her daughter Kelly has been possessed by a ghost. However, at the very start of the story, Ali does not have a problem – that only comes later, once Joan has taken over Kelly's body. So you might think this story does not follow the classic comedy story arc or even agree with the basic rules of womag stories.

But if you look at it again, you'll see that actually, it does. Try putting the ghost, Joan, centre stage, and summarising the story from her point of view:

Joan is a ghost, and she has a problem. She killed herself to be with her fiancé Jack who'd died on D-Day, but she can't find him. When a young girl moves into the house Joan haunts, Joan uses her to communicate with the living, and they are able to help reunite Joan with Jack.

I chose to use a living character as my narrator. But you can also use a ghost as narrator, and later on, I have an example of that.

Remember our three story types? This one is an example of Type 1 – a story where the ghost is the character with the problem, which must be resolved before the ghost can truly rest in peace. There are some 'rules' associated with this type of story. I use the word 'rule' guardedly as I have never believed in imposing rules on fiction – write what you like, how you like! But to make this type of ghost story *work*, and be publishable, it is worth considering the following points:

1. What is the ghost's problem? In other words, why is this ghost still hanging around on earth when they ought to be in heaven (or where ever it is souls go to rest in peace)? Joan's problem is that she can't find Jack.

2. Why is the ghost haunting the people *now*? What has happened to make it become active? In *We'll Meet Again* it is the arrival of seventeen year old Kelly in the house. Before then, Joan only haunted her sister, Betty. I like to imagine that Joan felt she could relate to Kelly because they were so close in age, and shared an interest in clothes, albeit rather different styles!

3. Decide on your ghostly rules. Can your ghosts move objects or not? Can they walk through walls or not? Be consistent. I'll talk more about this later in the book.

Just the three rules, that will do. There's a well-known 'rule of three' you can apply to writing. Lists of three work well. Three adjectives. Three examples. Three ways of using a metaphor. Did I have Kelly/Joan look at or buy three items from eBay? Yes – the brooch, the tea-dress, and the yellow blouse. Any more would have been too many. Any fewer wouldn't have made the point well enough. So I'll stick at just three rules for a Type 1 ghost story. And didn't I also have just three types of story? Spooky, this rule of three business, isn't it?

At the end of *We'll Meet Again* Joan's problem is resolved and she is reunited with Jack. Ali and Mike have got their daughter back, and Kelly has her body back, so their problems are also resolved. But I also think Gran's problem is resolved. She's spent over sixty years not talking about her little sister, to whom she was obviously close, because of the stigma her family attached to suicide in the 1940s. She's had chance to spend some time with that sister again, and also knows there's an afterlife to look forward to, when her time comes. I think one reason for the enduring popularity of ghost stories is our hope that there IS life after death; that the soul goes on. I'll explore this idea further, later on in the book.

The title of this story was suggested by a friend in a writing group who'd seen an early draft of this story. I am useless at thinking up titles. I knew instantly it was perfect, and indeed, *Take A Break* did not change it. Anyone reading this who's been published by *Take A Break* will know how rare it is for them to keep an author's original title!

It's some years since I wrote this story but I remember what inspired it. I started with the idea of someone buying only vintage items from eBay. I'd just bought myself a gorgeous 1940s diamante brooch, and had browsed through the vintage jewellery and clothing sections. Then I went on a 'what if?' spree. You know, what if you could only see vintage items, because you were being controlled or manipulated by a ghost? What if that ghost wanted you to buy only things it liked? What if the ghost took over completely? You've just read the result.

Settings

As with any womag story – in fact, any short story or even novel – the setting is very important. In *We'll Meet Again* most of the action is in fairly run-of-the-mill settings, a 1930s semi and an old people's home. The WW2 cemetery is more unusual. Settings, used well, can almost become a character in their own right. They'll certainly lend atmosphere and colour to your story. It's too easy sometimes to start writing, especially if you're starting with dialogue, and get half way down the page before you realise you haven't actually put your characters anywhere. Then you get lazy and stick them in the kitchen drinking coffee. Unless there's a good reason for them being in the kitchen, try to think of somewhere more interesting and relevant to your story's theme for them to have the conversation. In a car stuck in a traffic jam? While walking home in the rain after taking the kids to school? While queuing up to take their turn at the church fete's tombola?

If you can think up a really unusual setting for your ghost story, it will help it stand out and should improve your chances of publication. I once set a ghost story in a swimming pool… actually, let's have a look at that one now. It's another Type 1 story, first published in *Take A Break's Fiction Feast* in 2009.

Play With Me

Play with me! The voice sounded crystal clear. A child, a little girl, desperate for a playmate.

I surfaced, confused, and shook my head to clear the water from my ears. Who had I heard? I looked around for the owner of the voice but there were no children nearby, just a couple of adults swimming lengths. My son, Lewis, was splashing around in the shallow end of the pool. Besides, how could I have heard any voice clearly while swimming underwater? I must have been imagining it. I swam down the pool to join Lewis.

'Mum, teach me to dive, like you promised!' He was only seven, but already he was an excellent swimmer. He'd had lessons since he was four and it had paid off. Now that the King George V Baths had reopened, so close to our home, I'd be able to take him swimming even more often. And he was right; I had promised him I'd teach him to dive.

'Come on then,' I called to him. 'Race you up to the deep end!' I gave him a head start, then swam after him.

This was a beautiful swimming pool. It had stood empty and derelict for thirty years, preserved from the developers by a Grade 2 listing, because of its wonderful Art Deco styling. Eventually with the help of a lottery grant it had been restored and reopened. Lewis and I were among the first visitors.

We climbed out of the pool using the deep-end steps, and stood on the edge.

'OK, Lewis. Watch me,' I said. I stood straight and tall, arms stretched upwards then raised up onto my toes and dived in. Not bad, I thought, as I entered the water clean and straight.

Nice dive! Play with me? That voice again. There was something familiar about it. Apart from having heard it under water before, I mean. Some long buried memory…

I pushed up from the bottom of the pool, and emerged to a grinning Lewis. 'That was fab, Mum! Teach me, now!'

'OK,' I said. 'Start by sitting on the edge, then roll yourself over and in.' He did, then came up giggling. 'The water went up my nose, Mum! First to touch the bottom, ready, Go!' He took a deep breath and duck-dived. I followed.

Play with me.

Janie. Now I knew where I'd heard the voice before. She'd been in my class in infants' school, thirty years ago. I remembered guiltily how she'd called me her best friend, but I'd always brushed her off, promising her I'd play with her later. I never did, though.

Hello, Karen. Play with me?

I kicked to the surface, shaking. Why did I keep hearing Janie's voice under the water? I hadn't seen her since… since she died. She'd drowned. I remembered now. We'd only been about six at the time. They'd closed this pool soon after.

Lewis. Where was he? I looked around, but couldn't spot him. Had he swum to the other end? Had he even come back up from the bottom? I took a gulp of air and went back under the water. There he was – at the bottom of the pool, kicking frantically, his eyes panicked behind his goggles. I swam down to him to help him to the surface, but something was holding him down. No matter how hard I pulled, he was held fast.

I want him, Karen. To play with.

The water around Lewis seemed different to the rest of the pool. More viscous, slightly clouded. I could make out arms, tightly wrapped around my son, and a face, close to his.

Let go of him!

Janie seemed able to hear my thoughts.

No. I won't let go. I want to play.

I pulled Lewis again but couldn't move him. I needed help, and quickly. I kicked to the surface and shouted but the lifeguard was at the other end of the pool talking to some misbehaving teenagers. It was up to me to save Lewis.

Taking a huge breath I dived down again. Lewis's struggles were weaker now, and I knew I didn't have long.

Janie, listen. I sent my thoughts towards her as clearly as I could. Let go of Lewis. Let him go up. You come too – I'll play with you up there, out of the water. Let him go, please!

But you're too old for me now, Karen. I want to play with this boy. He can be my best friend. Not you. You didn't like me.

I'm sorry, Janie.

Then I heard Lewis's voice, in my head: I'll play with you. I'll be your friend.

Promise?

Lewis's eyes flickered and closed. Lewis! I caught him under his arms, braced my feet against the bottom and pulled once more. My lungs were bursting with the effort. At that moment the lifeguard plunged in beside us and grabbed him too.

Pull me up, too.

OK, Janie. You too.

Suddenly it was easy, and we shot to the surface. The lifeguard hauled Lewis out of the pool, where he instantly began coughing and spluttering.

As I climbed out of the pool to go to him I felt a small hand on my arm. The water clouded slightly, taking, for a second, the shape of a little girl. Then the shape dispersed and a mist formed briefly above the surface. *Thank you.*

I rushed to Lewis, and gathered him into my arms. 'Oh my darling, thank goodness you're OK,' I gasped.

'Where is she, Mum? The girl who wanted to play?'

'She's gone, darling. You're safe now.' I stroked his hair and kissed his forehead.

'She just wanted a friend, Mum,' said Lewis.

I squeezed my beautiful, caring son, and hoped with all my heart that Janie would find true friendship, wherever she was now.

Her voice sounded in my head one last time. *I'm not gone. I'm up here now. You pulled me up, and now I'm free. I can play anywhere now, with anyone…*

Janie's voice grew distant. I heard a final, faint little giggle, and then silence.

The End

Play With Me – Discussion

Now that I read this one through again, I've realised it's almost identical in structure to *We'll Meet Again,* although the setting and characters could hardly be more different. It's definitely a Type 1 story – a ghost with a problem which is stopping her from being able to rest in peace. In this case we've got little Janie, who drowned, and has been unable to leave the swimming pool – perhaps because it's been closed since she died there. She wants nothing more than a playmate. From her point of view, the boy who dives to the bottom of the pool is about her age and would make a perfect playmate, so she holds him down. At the end, she allows herself to be pulled up to the surface along with the boy, and this sets her free from the pool, so she can go and play anywhere.

Look back at the 'rules' for a Type 1 story: the ghost must have a problem; the ghost must have a reason for haunting the people *now*; and there must be consistent rules about what the ghost can and cannot do.

Janie is haunting Karen now because the pool has only just been reopened, after thirty years of lying disused and derelict. And she knows Karen from her school days.

Janie can move in the water but cannot get out of the pool without some help. She can speak inside Karen's and Lewis's head, and can read their minds. It's OK to have ghosts be able to do whatever you want them to, as long as you are consistent about it throughout the story.

There's a sinister tone in parts of this one – we imagine that Janie wants Lewis dead so he can be her playmate. She's trying to drown him, just as she herself drowned. And you know what, when I first wrote this story, for my writing class competition, poor little Lewis did die. The story ended with him lying limp in his mother's arms. I think I won that competition, then stupidly sent the story off to *Take A Break* as it was. I got a reply from the fiction editor, saying she liked it but the ending was 'too awful' and could I please change it so the boy didn't die? Of course I changed it immediately to the ending reproduced above; sent it back within a couple of days and sold it. It's *vitally important* if you want to sell your stories not to be too precious about them. Never refuse to change something to suit a market, how ever much you might love your original. The editors know their markets. They know what their readers will like, and they will only buy fiction which fits with their magazine's style.

You've read the section about story arcs in my introduction, and so you'll realise immediately that if Lewis dies, then for Karen and Lewis the story does not follow the comedy arc. OK, for Janie we can argue that it does, but to be a successful womag story the MC needs to end up in a better place. And I think she does – she finally has some sort of closure.

Karen was mean to Janie when they were children, perhaps she even bullied her. Had this story been longer, say 2000 words (it is just 1000 words and fitted on one page in the magazine), I would have built on this, and given Karen more of a sense of guilt at the way she had treated Janie as a child. Perhaps her bullying indirectly led to Janie's death? At the end of the story, Janie is free to play, and has thanked and presumably forgiven Karen for how she was treated during her childhood.

This idea came to me when I was swimming lengths in my local pool one day. I'd let my mind wander. Lengths can be so boring. By the time I left the pool the story was more or less fully formed in my head. I went home, jotted down a few notes, and wrote the story a couple of days later. I love those stories which arrive almost all at once! Writing them is like taking dictation. (Who from, I wonder? Cue spooky music…) Sadly, it doesn't always happen like that, and other stories have to be dragged out of me, word by word, kicking and screaming.

Coming To Terms

In *Play With Me*, Karen gets some sort of closure for Janie's death, and as I said above I would have expanded on this element if the story had been longer (it was originally written for my writing class competition which imposed a limit of 1000 words). Expanded, this story might have become a hybrid of a Type 1 and Type 2 story.

A reminder of what a Type 2 story is: A story in which the ghostly presence helps the MC come to terms with a loss, usually the loss of who ever the ghost was when it was alive. 'Coming to terms' is another way of saying 'closure' (and is perhaps a more British phrase than the American term closure.)

Let's look at a Type 2 story now. They're completely different, as I hope you'll see from this example.

Footprints In The Sand

Carolyn headed to the water's edge, and kicked off her flip-flops. She turned towards the setting sun, and paddled along the beach where the gentle surf met drier sand. The water cooled her feet and calmed her nerves. Shaking her hair free of its band, she relished the way the light summer breeze played with its ends, lifting her spirits. She looked back towards where Ian was sitting, and watched as the waves washed away her footprints. If only all her worries could be washed away as easily.

It had been a tough week. The toughest yet. Mel's funeral was over a month ago now, but Carolyn still missed her sister with every breath she took. And Ian wasn't helping. Whenever she allowed a few tears to slip, he sighed with exasperation, and shook his head.

'Pull yourself together, Caro,' he snapped. 'She's gone, and you have to get used to it. What would she think of you snivelling for weeks like this?'

Carolyn had begun biting her lip to stop the tears when Ian was around, and crying quietly and cathartically by herself when he was out. They'd been married for twenty-three years but since the children had left home Carolyn felt she'd grown apart from him. They didn't really have much in common any more.

Take now, for example. Ian had come with her to the beach under sufferance. He was sitting on a deckchair on the prom, reading a paper with a scowl on his face. It was a beautiful day, but Carolyn knew he'd rather be at home, watching football with the curtains drawn against reflections on the TV screen.

She wondered if she'd ever have the courage to leave him. She wished Mel was here to advise her. All her life she'd followed in the footsteps of her older sister, only going her own way after talking things through with Mel. Since Mel's untimely death, Carolyn felt lost and alone.

An uneven wave pulled back, leaving just one of her footprints. She drew a square around it with her toe. As children, she and Mel had spent hours on this same beach, playing follow-the-leader and hopscotch. Mel always went first, and Carolyn would be careful to hop exactly in her sister's footprints.

She smiled as she remembered how Mel would make ever bigger steps, till poor Carolyn struggled to jump between them. 'Hurray, you win!' Mel would laugh, if Carolyn managed to complete the course without making any footprints of her own.

She wiped away a tear as she remembered how the pattern set in childhood had been followed into adulthood. She was three years younger than Mel, and had done everything – first boyfriend, 'A' levels, summer job in a hotel, nursing training, husband, two children – exactly three years after Mel did them.

But Mel had forged a new career after her children were grown. She'd started up a nursing agency, which had become a real success.

Her husband Joe had supported her – even doing some of the agency's admin. Mel had asked Carolyn if she'd like to take over the admin role.

'You'd love it, Caro,' she'd said. 'And it would leave me more time to get out and about drumming up more business. Talk to Ian about it if you must, but do say yes!'

Carolyn had talked to Ian. 'No way!' he'd said. 'Bad idea to work for your sister. Anyway, it'd take all your time, and I'd end up eating ready-meals for tea. I'm not having that. You stay at home where you belong.'

At the funeral, Joe talked about closing the agency. 'It's a shame,' he said. 'Mel would have loved it to continue, but I'm not qualified to run it full time.'

Carolyn had been too upset to even think about it. She'd lost her sister, her best friend, her confidante, her inspiration.

Now, walking along the beach, she once again felt a wave of grief. Mel had been fifty-six. Too young to die in a random road accident. She held her face in her hands and sobbed. 'Why did you have to go, Mel? How am I going to cope, with Ian, without you here to help me?'

The sea lapped at her skirt, bringing her back to the present. Ian was waving angrily at her from the prom. She guessed he was bored. But she couldn't go back to him now with tears rolling down her face. He'd only shout at her again. She needed to compose herself first. Giving a small, non-committal wave, she turned to walk westwards again to let the sun dry her tears.

There was a line of footsteps in the sand. Without thinking, she began placing her feet in them – they were a tiny bit bigger than her feet but just the right distance apart. The footsteps led away from Ian. How right that felt!

A wave washed over the footprints. Carolyn felt a pang of disappointment – she would no longer be able to step in them. But as the wave pulled back, she saw that the footprints were still there, as strongly defined as ever. They petered out a few metres along the beach, but as the next wave came and went, it left more footprints leading further along, further away from Ian.

'Is it you, Mel?' Carolyn whispered. 'Are you showing me the way?' The breeze in her hair sighed a yes, and another wave left more footprints, marching steadily along the beach and into the future.

And Carolyn now knew her path. Mel had shown her, once again. She would phone Joe, and ask if she could take over running the agency. If Ian didn't like that, well, Ian could go hang. Because she was going to leave him.

She would make her own way in life now. She'd trodden in Mel's footsteps for the last time. 'Thanks, Mel,' she whispered. 'I'll be all right now, I think.'

The breeze caressed her face then suddenly died down. Ahead, the footprints curved away from the sea and were lost in the soft sand. Carolyn took a deep breath of salty air, wiped her face and turned back to face Ian, and her future.

The End

Footprints in the Sand – Discussion

Well, that was different from the first two stories, wasn't it? We don't see the ghost or hear her speak. There is only a line of footprints, and a breeze around Carolyn's face.

This story fits the comedy story arc perfectly, from Carolyn's point of view. And hers is the *only* point of view I could use. She starts off in a bad place, unable to even begin to come to terms with the loss of her sister. There's a lot of back story, in which we see glimpses of the girls as children, and also see how their lives progressed as adults. We find out that Mel's loss is not Carolyn's only problem – she is in a loveless marriage with Ian, who won't let her do anything for herself. And the problems are resolved by the ghost of Mel leaving footprints in the sand, showing Carolyn the way ahead.

Back story. There's a lot of it in this one, and I think that's probably true of all Type 2 ghost stories. I've given this story quite a circular structure – it starts with Carolyn on the beach walking along and introduces her problems. Then we get all the back story explaining how she came to be there, with those problems. And then we return to the moment in time, on the beach, and the resolution.

I suppose it would be possible to tell this story in a linear way – start with Carolyn and Mel as children, fast-forward to them as nursing students, and again to their weddings to Ian and Joe, the arrival of their children, the gradual cooling of Carolyn and Ian's marriage, Mel's accident, the funeral, and then the trip to the beach.

What do you think, would that have worked? No. Because we'd have been bored stiff wondering what the point of the story was, right up until the last scene on the beach.

A womag story must always have a *point*. What will the reader take away from the story? What new understanding about life, the universe and everything will they have, now that they've read it? What fundamental truth does the story demonstrate? To be truly satisfying, all stories must have a point to make.

The *point* is what makes the difference between a story and an anecdote. An anecdote simply says, 'x happened.' A story says, 'x happened, which makes you think about y,' where y is the *theme* of the story. For our Type 1 ghost stories, the theme is life after death. Finding peace in the afterlife. Which is something we all want to believe in. For Type 2 stories, the theme is in the definition – coming to terms. These stories show that however painful it may be, it is possible to come to terms with a loss, and move on. You don't forget, but ultimately you owe it to your lost loved one to make the most of your own life.

So, by giving this story a circular structure, starting almost at the end, I've been able to hint to the reader what the point of the story will be, right at the start. Another way of looking at this is to consider your story's *hook*. The hook is what makes the reader want to continue, after they've read the first paragraph or two. Which implies the hook needs to be there in the first paragraph or two. I think the hook in *Footprints in the Sand* is the line: If only all her worries could be washed away as easily. What worries? The story goes on immediately to tell us.

Emotion is vitally important in coming to terms stories. In fact, get emotion by the bucket load into any story and you'll increase your chances of selling it. What emotion? Well, any emotion. Here, obviously, it's grief. (That's the problem with ghost stories. They tend to be about dead people.) When writing a story, think about what emotion your MC would be feeling, and get it on the page. Don't be afraid of putting too much emotion in your story – Della Galton always says to put in as much as you can and then double it. Tap into your own experiences to do this. I've never had a sister die – I've never even had a sister. But my Dad died some years back, and I can remember all too clearly how I felt. So if I'm writing grief, I go back there, and try to write from the heart. Makes me cry, of course, to write it. Sometimes your aim is to make your reader cry as well. They'll only cry reading it if you cried writing it. But don't forget to round it all off with an uplifting ending. Don't leave your poor readers in the depths of despair. Remember the comedy story arc at all times!

I gave you three rules for Type 1 stories, so I guess I should give you three possible rules for Type 2 stories as well. OK, here they are:

1. Use lots of emotion.

2. Use a circular structure, so there's a strong hook and the back story which is essential in these stories comes later or is drip-fed in.

3. The ghost is not the main point of the story.

I've already talked about rules 1 and 2, so that leaves rule 3. Here you need to ask yourself, could you tell this story without the ghost? Think back to the Type 1 stories – *We'll Meet Again* and *Play With Me*. They make no sense without the ghost. The ghost IS the story. But what about *Footprints in the Sand?* It would be easy to tell this one without the ghost. In fact, the ghost is barely there, and could even be just a figment of Carolyn's imagination. Those footsteps could be from some earlier beach walker, and she's just imagining that they're appearing after the wave pulls back.

Ghost stories with no ghost

You might think I'm stretching the definition here. Maybe you wouldn't class *Footprints in the Sand* as a ghost story at all. But I think it is. The next question to think about is how subtle can you go? How can you write a ghost story with no actual ghost? It might sound daft, but it's the only way to get 'ghost' stories into some of the womags. *Take A Break's Fiction Feast* regularly uses ghost stories, Type 1 and Type 2, usually three or so in each issue. But many other magazines probably wouldn't take a Type 1. (They might take Type 3, which we'll come to later.) However if you can write a subtle enough Type 2 story, you'll probably be able to sell it to any of the womags. Remember Type 2 stories are all about coming to terms, and include lots of emotion and back story.

The next story is the first one I ever sold, to *Woman's Weekly* back in 2004, not very long after I lost my Dad. And yes, I guess the two characters were based loosely on my Mum and me.

Golden Wedding

After the waiter had taken their orders, June sat back and looked across the table at her mother Margaret. It would have been Margaret's Golden Wedding anniversary today.

'So, Mum. How's your day been? Not too lonely I hope?'

'It's been an odd sort of day,' Margaret replied. 'I was pretty sad when I woke up this morning, of course. Actually, it was peculiar. My alarm clock didn't go off, I think the batteries must have run out. But the neighbour's dog barked loudly, just after eight, and that woke me.'

'What, Mrs Shepherd's dog? I've never known him to bark.'

'No, I've never heard him before. Anyway, it was fortunate he did bark, or I'd never have woken up. I had a hair appointment at nine and I'd have missed it . So I blew a kiss at Eddie's photo, said happy anniversary to him, and got up.'

'Oh, Mum, it must be so hard for you, today of all days.'

'Well yes, dear, but I mustn't be too sad. He wouldn't have liked that. Anyway I took my breakfast out to the conservatory because it was such a lovely morning. Oh, and you know that loose corner of vinyl on the kitchen floor?'

June nodded. She'd been trying to get hold of an odd-job man to go and fix it before her mother tripped over it.

'Well, I caught my foot in it. It's alright, I didn't fall, but I dropped my coffee cup. My favourite one, too. I thought it'd smash, but I must have knocked the oven glove off its peg at the same time, because the cup landed on the glove and didn't break.'

'That was lucky, Mum! I'll get someone to fix that flooring as soon as possible.'

The waiter brought their starters, melon for Margaret and potato skins with soured cream for June. A bit indulgent perhaps, but she felt like having some comfort food.

'Anyway, after I'd had my hair done,' continued Margaret between mouthfuls, 'I decided to go straight on to the shops. But I was just about to turn onto the dual carriageway when I remembered I had to collect that raffle money from Sheila. So I went through town instead, past Sheila's house. And I'm so glad I did, because on the radio news later it said there'd been a big accident on the dual carriageway, and the traffic had been stuck for hours.'

'Yes, I heard that too. Good job you didn't get caught up in it.'

'So I did my shopping, then you'll never guess what your silly old Mum did.'

'What?' June was amused.

'Well, I'd left my handbag at the hairdressers. I didn't realise until I was in the checkout queue. Then I remembered I had all that raffle money in the car. As you know I always keep the cash anyway, and pay a cheque into the WI account. So I used that to pay for the groceries. Lucky I had it!'

'Absolutely! Good thinking, Mum.'

The waiter cleared away the starters, and brought the main courses. Both had chosen pizza: Margaret had a Four Seasons, June's was an Americano with extra pepperoni.

'It was lovely weather this afternoon, wasn't it, Mum? Did you get a chance to do any gardening?'

'Oh yes, dear. I got plenty done. Weeded that long bed beside the fence, and dead-headed some of the roses. I did that lovely red 'Ruby Wedding' one – do you remember it, love? You bought that for me ten years ago to the day. And it looks better every year. I do wish your dad could have seen it today – it's got so many blooms on it.'

June sighed, recalling the big family party they'd had for her parents Ruby Wedding. Her father had joked about not having a golden wedding do – too expensive, he said. He'd like to be away on a cruise for the golden wedding, perhaps June would treat them? June had laughed, not likely on her salary, but she'd resolved to buy her parents the best golden wedding present she could afford. But Eddie had died just a month after their forty-ninth anniversary.

'So,' Margaret clearly hadn't finished recounting her day. 'I went back inside to make a cup of tea then I realised I was missing an earring. My lovely pearl drops, the last present Eddie ever gave me.'

'Oh no!'

'Well, I searched high and low, but I couldn't find it anywhere. Oh, I was so upset, June. So then I thought perhaps it had fallen off in the garden. I knew there'd be no hope of finding it – you know what my garden's like, at this time of year.'

June nodded. Margaret's garden was huge, probably too much for one elderly lady, and was a riot of flowers. Beautiful, wild and abundant with not a spare inch of soil anywhere.

'But, June, just as I was on my way out, Tibby stalked past me, tail in the air. He went to the 'Ruby Wedding' rose and started scratching. Oh no you don't, I told him. You go and do your business elsewhere, and I went over to shoo him away. And there it was.'

'What?'

'My earring, of course. Must have fallen off while I dead-headed the rose, and was nestling in one of the blooms. Tibby led me straight to it. Can you believe it?'

June grinned. Another piece of luck.

'And to top it all, I checked the mid-week lottery numbers just before you collected me this evening.'

'Oh my God, Mum, you haven't…'

'Just ten pounds, love. But it'll pay for our wine this evening won't it? Poor Eddie. He never won a penny on the lottery; he'd have been so excited. Oh, I do wish he could have been with me today.'

June smiled. 'You know, Mum, with all the luck you've had today, I think he was.' She raised her glass. 'Here's to Dad.'

Margaret lifted hers. 'Thanks, Eddie.'

The End

Golden Wedding – Discussion

When introducing this story I mentioned it was the first story I ever sold. For that reason it has a soft spot in my heart, and got included in this book. I'm not entirely sure *Woman's Weekly* would buy it now – their style has changed over the years. You should always study current issues of your chosen market to see what they are publishing *now*.

When I sold this story I showed it to my husband (who will only ever read my work *after* it's been published) and he pronounced it 'drivel'. Well, he's not exactly the target audience, is he? I wasn't hurt at all. He's incredibly supportive of my writing, and brings me lots of cups of tea to keep me going. What he *meant* to say was that it is very gentle, warm, and an everyday kind of story. (That's what 'drivel' means, in his lexicon, obviously.) Many readers would be able to relate to it – if you have a widowed parent, or a mother who prattles on about the minutiae of her life, or if you just miss someone who's no longer with us.

I count this as a Type 2 ghost story – was Eddie watching over his wife on this special day, and making sure things didn't go wrong for her? It's a comforting idea that perhaps he was. It's only a mildly 'coming to terms' story because both Margaret and June seem reasonably OK about their loss – they're certainly not wallowing in grief the way Carolyn is in *Footprints in the Sand*. But the first wedding anniversary after a spouse's death is always going to be a difficult milestone, which needs to be got through as well as possible, and that is what I was trying to get across.

Ghost stories work well as coming to terms stories, as we've seen. Why is this? What's the psychology behind the enduring popularity of ghost stories? The next section covers my thoughts on this. You may have different ideas, and I'd love to hear them!

Why do people like ghost stories?

Some people enjoy scary stories, the type that womag ghost stories aren't, for the same reason they enjoy horror films. There's a thrill (or so I understand – I hate horror myself) in being scared witless when you know you are completely safe. Bad things happen to other, fictional people, while you yourself are curled up on your sofa with a comforting fleece blanket tucked around you and a mug of hot chocolate in your hand. You experience the adrenalin rush, the thumping heart and sweaty palms, without having to actually run away from the monster yourself.

But as we've seen, womag ghost stories are different. You're unlikely to sell a story that is genuinely scary to any womag. So what is it about gentle ghost stories which appeals?

Let's look at Type 2 stories first, as I think their appeal is the most obvious to understand. They are, as I've said, a subset of 'coming to terms' stories. A ghostly presence, which may be real or imagined by the MC, helps the MC move on after the loss of a loved one.

These stories are always popular because readers can relate to them. Everyone has lost someone important in their life – whether a grandparent, beloved pet, friend, parent or God forbid, a child. It's possible to write coming to terms stories without a ghost, and indeed, I've seen plenty and written a few myself. I think adding a ghost, even a very subtle, barely-there one (footprints in the sand, coincidental good luck) can give them an extra dimension. It also plays into our innate desire to believe that there *is* life after death; that our lost loved ones aren't completely gone, and are still around in some form, watching over us and guiding us.

Many ancient cultures practised ancestor-worship. This grew out of that same, quintessentially human desire, to want to hold on to the memories of those departed. It's a sliding scale from believing your Dad is still there watching over you, to erecting totems in his honour, and passing legends of his greatness down to your children and their children, and on down the generations even when no one's left who remembers the living man. When we are children, if things go wrong we run to our parents to sort it out. When we're adults perhaps sometimes we still need to look to our departed parents or grandparents for advice. What would Granddad have done? What can I do which would have made Mum proud? There is a comfort to be had, if you believe that they're still around in some form, standing behind you, cheering you on throughout your life.

And maybe they are. You're a product of your ancestors, so there is a little bit of each of them in you. Perhaps when you experience ghosts of ancestors it is those parts of your subconscious mind coming to the fore.

What about Type 1 stories, where the MC is not grieving, and the ghost is not related to the MC? Well, I think the appeal here comes from that same desire to believe in an afterlife. There's still a comfort element – but this time we're thinking of our *own* mortality. Death is, after all, a tiny bit final. The body stops functioning, we put it in the ground or cremate it, and then that person is simply no longer there. It'll happen to us all, one day. But Type 1 ghost stories show us an afterlife. Souls of the departed staying on earth until they've resolved their problems, then moving on to wherever it is ghosts end up. Have you seen the film, *Ghost*, with Patrick Swayze and Demi Moore? That's a classic Type 1 ghost story. The endings of these tales are always incredibly satisfying. The ghost is happily laid to rest, and the living characters move on, having gained a little bit of knowledge or understanding about life after death.

By the way, it doesn't matter in the slightest whether you, the author, believe in ghosts or life after death or any of that shenanigans. All that matters is that you can put yourself in the shoes of someone, eg your MC, who *does* believe in it, and then tell a darn good story, following the 'rules' of the Type 1 ghost story.

Do *I* believe in ghosts? I'll let you know, later on in this book!

For readers who don't believe in ghosts, or magazine editors who think their readers don't believe in ghosts, you need to write a story which has an alternative rational explanation. And that leads us nicely onto a discussion of Type 3 stories.

Alternative Rational Explanation (A.R.E.)

In the introduction to this section, I defined Type 3 stories as those which included an A.R.E. The point of these stories is, I guess, to make you stop and wonder, *could* it have been a ghost? The story must be left open enough to allow you to decide either way.

We need an example to illustrate what I mean, don't we? Well, I have just the thing. This one is another I sold during my main ghost story writing spree of 2008-2009. It was first published in *Take A Break's Fiction Feast*, though actually when I was writing it, I had *My Weekly* in mind as its most likely market.

Still Here

'You still there?' Doris called through to the living room from where she was standing by the kitchen sink. 'Still there on that sofa? I suppose I'll have to eat my dinner by myself. As usual.'

She grumbled quietly to herself as she set the table in the kitchen. She laid two places, even though she knew only one would be used. Harold wouldn't be eating with her.

Her cat, Freddie, twined himself around her legs as she ate, and was rewarded with a few titbits.

'There, sweetie,' she said. 'You might as well have that bit of bacon rind. Leave that old man on the sofa, like always. Harold, love,' she called, raising her voice slightly, 'Freddie loves bacon rind, did you know that?'

She fondled the cat's ears affectionately. 'You're a good companion, you are, Freddie. Better than that old man of mine. You hear that, Harold? My Freddie's a better companion than you. What do you say to that, then?'

Silence. Harold clearly had nothing to say to it.

Doris finished her dinner and cleared away the plates.

Once the dishwasher was loaded, she sat for a few minutes at the kitchen table reading a magazine. Freddie jumped onto her lap, and curled up happily, purring loudly.

A few minutes later, Doris pushed the cat off her lap.

'Time to give our Jacqui a ring,' she said, hauling herself to her feet. She went to the phone in the hallway and dialled her daughter.

Jacqui answered straight away. 'Hi Mum,' she said. 'How are you?'

'I'm fine, love. Just finished my dinner. *He* didn't eat anything, of course. Just sat on the sofa while I ate. He's barely moved all day.'

'Good, Mum,' said Jacqui. 'I'm glad you're keeping the cat off the table now. You know I worry about hygiene when you feed him from your plate.'

'Oh, you mean Freddie! Er, well, I might have given him a few little bits. He does so like to keep me company when I eat, you know.'

'I thought you said he was on the sofa?'

'Oh no, love. But he wasn't on the table, before you scold me. He was under my chair.'

'Er, right.' Jacqui sounded confused as she changed the subject. 'So anyway, Mum, I'll be round on Saturday to take you shopping as usual. Is two o'clock OK for you?'

'That'll be fine, love. I'll make sure we've had our lunch before then.'

'Lunch? I reckon you're feeding that cat too much, Mum.'

'No I'm not. Only half a tin in the mornings and some crunchies at night. See you Saturday, love.'

'OK Mum. See you then.'

Doris put the phone down and bent to stroke Freddie. 'She thinks I feed you too much, now. She should stop complaining. It was her who gave you to me, anyway. Remember, Freddie?'

Jacqui had chosen Freddie from a cat rescue centre. She'd appeared at the door one day a few weeks ago, with a bundle of black fur in an old cat basket.

'He's called Freddie. He'll be company for you, Mum,' she'd said. 'I don't like to think of you on your own.'

Doris hadn't exactly thought of herself as being on her own at that point, but even so she welcomed Freddie into her home. And she had to admit, her daughter was right. The cat was good company for her.

She sighed, remembering a time when she and Harold had discussed getting a pet. At that time, years ago, it was Doris who'd wanted a cat, but Harold had said no.

'Why would you want a cat when I'm still here?' he'd said. 'And you know, my darling, I'll always be here for you.'

Doris had hugged him tightly. 'I know you will, love. I know.' And so she never had owned a cat, until the day Jacqui had turned up on the doorstep with Freddie in a basket.

Freddie brought her abruptly back to the present, purring and winding himself through and around her legs.

'Watch out, Freddie! You'll have me tripping head over heels!' Doris took a step backwards, just as Freddie decided to rub himself around the back of her calves.

She wobbled, threw out her hands to steady herself and knocked over a jardinière. She crashed to the floor, along with her oversized rubber plant and landed amid shards of broken plant stand.

'Oh, oh, my hip!' Doris tried to roll over and get up, but the pain was too much. 'Harold! Oh Harold, love, help me!'

Freddie came over and rubbed himself against her shoulder. 'Freddie, you're a comfort, but not much use now. Oh, Harold, I wish you could help me!'

Freddie gave her a gentle lick on her cheek, and curled himself up against her shoulder. Doris reached up to stroke him, then noticed her phone, on its little table three feet above.

'If only I could reach that phone. I could call Jacqui...' She tried to pull herself over to it but it was no use. She couldn't move her left leg and the pain was so intense she thought she would pass out.

'Harold!' she called again, more feebly now. 'Harold, get off the sofa and help me, my love.'

But the sofa was empty.

The next thing Doris was aware of was the sound of a key in the lock. She opened her eyes and shook her head to wake herself up, then remembered where she was as pain shot up from her hip.

'Mum? Where are you, Mum? Oh no, Mum!' Jacqui rushed over to kneel beside her mother. 'What happened, Mum? I'll call an ambulance. Lie still.'

'I can't do much else, love. I think I must have tripped over the cat.' Doris listened while her daughter called an ambulance.

'There, Mum. They'll be here in a few minutes. Thank goodness I popped round!'

'Yes, love. Is it Saturday already? Have I been here two days?'

'No, Mum. It's Thursday evening. I spoke to you just half an hour ago. And then you rang again.'

'I didn't ring you. After I fell, I couldn't reach the phone. I just laid here, and dear old Freddie kept me company.'

'Well, my phone did ring,' said Jacqui. 'I answered it, but there was no one there. So I dialled 1471 to see who had called – if it was a nuisance call I was going to report it. And it was your number, so I rushed round. Thank goodness I did!'

'But I didn't ring,' Doris protested.

'Must have been Freddie, then,' said Jacqui decisively. 'Somehow he must have stepped on the last number redial button. Clever old thing! Hey, I think I heard the ambulance.' She got up to open the door.

Doris looked up at the phone. It was still in its place, with the receiver on its hook. Clever Freddie indeed, if he could lift the receiver, step on the button and then replace the receiver again afterwards.

But if it wasn't Freddie, that only left one option. She looked again at the phone. The cord was neatly wound around the base, in a way Doris hadn't seen since… since her beloved Harold had died.

She twisted her head to peek through the living room door at the empty sofa.

'Thanks, Harold,' she whispered. 'I knew you were still here, just like you promised. Stay till I get home again, and look after Freddie for me, my love.'

The End

Still Here – Discussion

So, did Freddie the cat press the Last Number Redial button, or did Harold the ghost stir himself from the sofa to make the call? Jacqui thinks it was the cat, Doris knows it was Harold. The reader can choose who to agree with.

When writing this type of ghost story, it's important to leave the story open-ended enough that either explanation could be the right one. And it really helps to have two characters, each picking a different explanation for the 'ghostly' events. That way your characters can put the two explanations across, rather than having you the author do it using some kind of omniscient view point.

I must admit, I find Type 3 stories more difficult to write than Type 1 ghost stories. You have to work hard to come up with the A.R.E. and for me, they're just not as much fun to write. Type 2 stories can be hard to write as well, because of all that emotion you need – especially if you are tapping into your own experiences of loss. They can leave you strung out by the time you type 'The End'. Type 3 stories need plenty of brain power. You have to come up with the usual characters and plot, and on top of that you've got to think of the A.R.E. and also, make sure the whole thing is not too contrived. That's a real danger with Type 3 stories.

With any fiction, after you've written it, it is always worth putting it aside for a week or two before coming back for the final edit. I think this is especially true of Type 3 ghost stories. With a bit of distance you'll spot anything that looks at all contrived. You'll also notice if you've given too much weight to one of the explanations, and perhaps need to balance it out a bit more.

Think of these stories as weighing scales, with the ghostly explanation on one pan and the A.R.E. on the other. In *Still Here*, Freddie and Harold must balance each other exactly for the story to work and appeal to both ghost-believers and non-believers. Did I get the balance right? I'm not sure. I think Harold's side of the scales may be a bit heavier than Freddie's. (All that stuff about the phone cord! In any case, who has phones with cords these days?) I sold the story to *Take A Break*, which is always happy to publish all types of ghost story, and doesn't much care about A.R.E.s. But had I tried its luck with *My Weekly*, I might well have changed the ending slightly so that the scales were better balanced.

You'll see from that last sentence, that a ghost story which might sell to one womag may not be suitable for another. A mistake beginner writers often make is to lump all womags into one pot, and assume that a story originally aimed at *Take A Break*, where a divorcée murders her ex-husband and buries his body in the garden before going off on a drinking spree with her hunky toy-boy, might also sell to The *People's Friend*. It won't. You need to study your markets, and understand the differences between them. Each womag takes a different type of story.

It's often possible to edit a story rejected by its original intended market so that it's suitable for another – as I would have with *Still Here*, changing its end. It was pleasing to sell this story to the first magazine I sent it to. However, this was not the first version of the story, by any means.

Never throw anything away

Years before, I'd written an earlier version, which I never tried to sell, knowing it wasn't suitable womag material. Then, during my 2008 ghost story-writing frenzy, I came across that original story and thought, hey, unsuitable structure but the idea's not half bad. Can I rewrite it? And it *was* a complete rewrite, not an edit. I started with a blank Word document and the printed original laid out beside me for reference. Here's that original story, which I've included to demonstrate the difference between a fine idea that would never sell, and a finished successful womag story. You see, it's not the idea that sells; it's the way you write it.

Companion
(Original version of Still Here)

So, George, as I was saying, they bought us the cat for company. Quite sweet of the kids really, when you think about it. They worry about us, now we're getting older, living here alone. I tell them they shouldn't worry – we're perfectly all right, aren't we? You and I, mooching along together, just as we always did, perfectly happy. Maybe not as happy as we were last year, but you can't have everything, eh George?

It was Carrie's idea. 'Mum, what about a cat?' she said.

'What about one?' I said.

'From the animal shelter,' she said. 'For company.'

And next thing I knew, she turned up on the doorstep with a bag of cat gear and a bundle of black and white fur. Oh, it was a surprise, wasn't it? I thought it was all just talk. I didn't know she would actually go ahead and get us a cat. Did you know she was doing it?

Well anyway, he's quite a sweet little thing. I've called him Pongo. Yes George, I know that's the name of the dog in *101 Dalmations*, but when you look at his markings he's a bit like a feline version of a spotty dog.

That's what Carrie used to call them, do you remember? She was mad about spotty dogs. She took that stuffed one to bed with her every night until it disintegrated.

Simon's the one who chose the basket and food bowl and all the other accessories – he told me so. You can tell they were bought by a man. He left all the price tags on. And Carrie wouldn't have gone for that boring brown bowl. She'd have picked out something a bit prettier, something cute perhaps. But it does the job, so I won't complain. Nice that the kids worked together on this isn't it? When you think how they argued and fought when they were teenagers. They've grown up into such lovely people. We did well there, you and me, bringing those two up. And I believe they've grown closer, this last year.

Pongo's about five years old, she said. He was found wandering around a cottage after his elderly owner died. Did I tell you that before? All scrawny and ragged he was. They don't know how long he'd gone without food, but the old lady had been dead at least a week when they found her, apparently. Incredibly loyal, wasn't he? I'd have thought a cat would just go off in search of somewhere better to live if it wasn't being fed at home. But our Pongo had stayed put with his owner, bless him.

Would he do that for us, do you think? Bit morbid to think about it, I suppose, but I can't help it. I mean, if something happened... he'd stay here and guard us, wouldn't he? I kind of like the idea. We wouldn't be left alone. He's settled in so quickly with us. Always mewing for his food, jumping onto my lap for a cuddle in the evenings. Oh, he's a good lad, my Pongo.

And you like him too, don't you George?

Gosh, there's the phone. Who's ringing us at this hour? Ooh, my old bones. I'm coming, hold on. Wish you could answer it sometimes, George, save my old knees.

'Hello?'

'Mum, hi.'

'Oh hello, Carrie!'

'How is he, then?'

'Ah, he's fine. Lying on the sofa. He didn't bat an eyelid when the phone went – left me to get it. He'll be listening in, though, you can bet on it.'

'Great, sounds like he's happy, then.'

'Oh yes, he's always happy…'

'Always? Mum, you've only had him two days…'

'Oh, the cat. Yes, he's quite content. Settled in nicely.'

'That's good. I just wanted to check… Listen Mum, I'll come round at the weekend, OK?'

'That'll be nice, dear. Look, it's late, we were about to go to bed so I must go…'

'You letting the cat sleep on your bed? Ah Mum. Think of all the cat hairs…'

'What, dear? No, I don't let Pongo upstairs.'

'OK, well that's probably best. Bye then, Mum, see you Saturday'

'Bye, love.'

It was Carrie, George. She was checking up on us again. Are we happy, is the cat on the bed, that sort of thing. Nice that she worries but sometimes, oh dear me, she fusses a bit too much. She was here just two days ago, after all. And she'll be back on Saturday. I'll have to get a joint in, she'll be expecting a decent dinner. Well, Pongo can have any leftovers, I suppose. What will he like best, do you think, chicken or a bit of beef?

So come on then, old man. Stir yourself, it's time for bed. Up you get, and up them stairs. Don't think I can't see you, making that face at me! Here, I'll give you what-for for that! Ooh, I'd chase you, I would, if my old knees would take it. Ooh, I'll be after you anyway, you cheeky old fella…. Pongo! Mind or I'll trip. Get away you daft cat…

George? George? What happened? How long have I been lying here? Oh my goodness, I tripped over the cat, didn't I? Oh, oh, I can't move…my hip…ooh that does hurt!

Oh dear me, George. What are we going to do? You can't use the phone, can you? And I can't move…

Pongo, there's no use mewing at me. I can't feed you from here, can I? Are you going to stay, keep me company till someone comes, then? Carrie'll be here Saturday. How many days until Saturday? Stay with me, Pongo. Come and lie beside me, that's right, you're a good cat, a real comfort.

Oh George, I do miss you. What did you have to go and leave me for? Leaving me all alone like this. I never thought I'd be the one left alone. Never thought you'd go first…

Oh I do feel unwell, I'll close my eyes for a moment…

'Mum? MUM! Oh God, Mum, are you all right? What happened?'

'Carrie? Is that you? Oh thank goodness. I've been here ages, I can't move.'

'I'm calling an ambulance. You'll be OK, Mum, just lie still. Here, lift your head and I'll put this cushion under it.'

'Thanks love, that's better. I tripped over the cat, you know. Then I couldn't move. Pongo's been a love, he's stayed with me all the time. I think I've slept most of it – it didn't feel like four days.'

'Four days? You've not been there four days, Mum. I was talking to you on the phone only an hour ago, remember? You were about to go to bed so we didn't chat long.'

'It's not Saturday then?'

'Goodness, no. It's still Tuesday evening.'

'So why are you here?'

'That's the strange part. The phone rang. I answered it, but there was no one there. My caller-id display showed your number, and I was worried, so I came straight over. Must have been the cat, I suppose. Knocked the receiver off the hook and stood on the Last Number Redial button, I guess.'

'Good old Pongo. So faithful, bless him.'

'I can hear the ambulance, Mum. I need to leave you for a moment, just to open the door and tell them where you are… won't be a minute….'

She's a good girl, our Carrie. Thank goodness she came straight over. But I can see the phone from here, and the receiver is still on the hook. Pongo would be able to knock it off, but not replace it, I don't think. And the curly wire is wrapped neatly the long way around the phone, just the way George always used to leave it.

Well I don't know how you managed it, George, but you did it. Thank you, my love. I guess I won't be seeing you again just yet, after all. But when I do, ah George, when we're together again, I'll thank you properly, my love.

The End

Companion – Discussion

What do you think? Which version do you prefer – *Still Here* or *Companion*? The earlier version – *Companion* – is mostly a monologue, with bits of dialogue between the unnamed old lady and her daughter thrown in. Monologues (from the Greek words meaning single speech) *can* be sold to some womags but probably not *Take A Break*. And I don't think this one as it stands would have sold anywhere, as its structure is too muddled, although it strikes me it would be easy to convert it into a radio play.

Having said that, monologues are great fun to write because they help you to really get inside your character's head. Once you get going, they usually pour out of you. Writing a monologue is a great way to get to know your character, perhaps in advance of writing a story about them. It can definitely help you establish a 'voice' for your story. I quite like the old lady's voice in *Companion*. She reminds me of my grandmother.

That's the great thing about writing ghost stories – you can bring the dead back to life. In fact, writing a Type 2 ghost story can be quite cathartic. I wrote one once where a ghostly father keeps saving his daughter from mishap. In the end, she's missing him so much she almost throws herself off a cliff. But he appears beside her and tells her it's not her time. She then gets back in her car and looks in the mirror, and sees her Dad's eyes looking back at her. He's not gone – he's a part of her and always will be, and finally she realises she can move on. This was one of the first ghost stories I wrote, and I sent it to *My Weekly*. It was rejected very gently with the comment that 'it read too much like a therapeutic tool for the writer'.

Use writing as catharsis – to help you deal with grief or anger. It definitely works. Write from the heart. But do try to distinguish the ones which are purely you working through your emotions from those which will have a broader appeal. There's a reason I haven't included that Dad story in this book. The *My Weekly* editor was far too perceptive.

From cats to dogs

Ooh, I was getting a bit heavy back there, wasn't I? Let's lighten the tone. Does your ghost have to be human? Just as an unusual setting might help sell your story, an unusual ghost could too. See what you think of this one.

What's Up With Benjy?

'Where's Benjy's bowl?' Sam shouted, from the utility room.

'Where it always is,' Abbie called in reply, wondering why he couldn't just open his eyes and search for it himself. She was busy washing up. As if in agreement Benjy came whining around her legs, looking up at her with doleful brown eyes.

'Daddy's feeding you,' she told him, fondling his floppy Spaniel ears. He nuzzled her hand and woofed happily. 'If he can find your bowl, that is.'

'Got it,' Sam came into the kitchen brandishing the bowl. 'It was out by the woodpile again. Why'd you move it?'

'I didn't. Perhaps Benjy pushed it out there?'

'Don't think so. He's been lazing on the hearth rug all afternoon.'

Abbie frowned, but turned back to the washing up. That was the third time in a week Benjy's bowl had mysteriously moved outside. And she'd heard barking from the garden when Benjy was out for a walk with Sam. Add to that, Benjy's sudden reluctance to go anywhere near the woodpile, and Abbie was beginning to feel spooked in her own home.

They'd bought the house a year before. It was a probate sale – the old lady who'd owned it had died and left it to her son. Sam and Abbie thought it was perfect, with its long, well-fenced garden for Benjy to play in, three bedrooms and cosy lounge with an open fireplace. The woodpile they'd inherited was an added bonus – enough logs to keep them in firewood for a couple of years at least.

But they'd underestimated how quickly well-seasoned wood burns, and by the end of the winter there wasn't much left. Abbie asked Sam to tidy it the following weekend.

Benjy wouldn't even go out in the garden on Saturday while Sam worked to restack the logs. He cowered in the living room, behind the sofa, whining occasionally. Abbie wondered if she should take him to the vet, but he perked up immediately when she fetched his lead and mentioned the magic word, 'walk'.

When they got back, Sam had finished tidying the wood. Benjy raised his hackles as soon as he entered the house. Abbie went through to the kitchen, where her husband was sitting with a cup of tea.

'Come on, Benj. I'll find you a biscuit,' she said. But he growled slightly, and slunk off to the living room.

'What's up with him? Is he all right?' asked Sam.

'He was fine on the walk. Don't know why he won't come in here now. What's this?' Abbie picked up a small picture in a battered old wooden frame which was lying on the kitchen table.

'I found it tucked between two of the logs. Do you think it's her – Mrs McKenzie – the old lady who lived here before us?'

The photo showed an elderly woman, her hand on the collar of a beautiful golden retriever, which was looking up at her with adoration.

'Could be,' Abbie said, peering closely at it. 'Are those teeth marks on the frame?'

'Well, it's certainly seen better days,' he replied. She handed the picture back, and Sam flipped open the kitchen bin and tossed it in.

Benjy wouldn't go into the kitchen for the rest of the day. Sam even had to put his food bowl down in the hallway. It was only later that evening, when Abbie had cleaned up after dinner and emptied the kitchen bin into the dustbin outside, that the dog ventured in. He crept cautiously around the edge of the room, sniffing the air. Whatever it was that had bothered him had clearly gone, and after circling the room he relaxed and settled down beside the still-warm oven.

'Do you think it's the photo he didn't like?' Abbie asked her husband. 'He wouldn't go near the woodpile when it was there, and he wouldn't come in the kitchen while it was in here.'

'Don't be daft,' Sam laughed. 'He never even saw it. And he always used to be OK near the woodpile, until last week. That photo must have been there since before we moved in.'

He was right. Still, Abbie could think of no other explanation.

That night, they were woken by a terrible bang. Benjy, who had been sleeping at the foot of the bed, began growling.

'What was that?' asked Sam.

'I don't know. We'd better check it out, though.'

They both pulled on dressing gowns, and crept downstairs, with Benjy following. There was no one there, to Abbie's relief. The sound had come from near the back door. Sam armed himself with the poker before opening it. Benjy stayed just inside, growling quietly. Outside, the wheelie bin was on its side, and its contents were strewn right across the driveway.

'Good grief! How on earth did that happen?'

'A fox?' suggested Abbie.

'No, a fox couldn't knock it over. Must have been a burglar, or a vandal. Thank goodness the doors were all secured.'

'What would a burglar want with our rubbish?' The idea of anyone poking around in their bin in the middle of the night freaked Abbie out.

'Identity theft? I'll have a word with the police in the morning. Let's have a cup of tea and get back to bed, love.'

Neither of them slept again that night. Even Benjy was restless, and kept pacing up and down. Abbie considered making him go down to the kitchen, but his presence was comforting. Not that he made much of a guard dog, though, she thought.

In the morning, Sam went out to clear up the rubbish in the driveway. He came back inside looking shaken.

'Abbie, this sounds mad, but something really odd has happened.'

'What?'

'I've just found that picture again. The one of the old woman and the dog. It's back in the woodpile, tucked between two logs just like it was before.'

Abbie sat down. This was all getting just a bit too spooky for comfort.

'There's something weird about that photo. Maybe it's, I don't know, haunted or something. Whatever it is, Sam, I want it out of here. If we can't throw it out with the rubbish we have to find another way to be rid of it.'

'I agree,' Sam said. 'I was thinking about it last night. Let's take it round to Peter McKenzie's. I've still got his forwarding address somewhere. I bet the photo is of his mum. We can give it back to him.'

Benjy had to be left at home. He simply could not be persuaded to climb in the car, not after Abbie had got in with the photo in her bag.

Abbie felt nervous, calling at the house of a complete stranger to hand over a tatty old photo. But Peter McKenzie turned out to be friendly and welcoming. As soon as Sam said who they were, he invited them in and made a pot of tea. When she pulled out the photo he laughed.

'That old picture! I wondered where it had gone. Poor Goldie, she looked for it everywhere when I first brought her here.'

'Goldie? Is that the dog in the photo?' asked Sam.

'Yes, Mum's dog. She was a funny old thing. So loyal, you know. Mum wouldn't let her come upstairs, and poor Goldie used to whine all night, shut up in the kitchen. So Mum gave her that photo. She rubbed her hands over it every evening so it smelt of her. Goldie kept it in her basket and slept with it every night.'

'How sweet!' said Abbie.

'Where did you find it?' asked Peter. 'I collected Goldie and all her gear when Mum had to go into hospital, but the photo wasn't there.'

'It was in the woodpile. Tucked between two logs,' said Sam.

'Of course! She often used to hide it there, if Mum was washing her bedding. I should have checked, but things were so hectic, and frankly, Goldie's photo wasn't my highest priority at that time.'

He looked out of the window for a moment, and sighed. 'But I don't understand. Why bring it back now? You must have been in the house over a year. In fact, why bring it back at all? It's pretty tatty – you can't have thought I'd want it?'

Abbie exchanged a glance with Sam. How could she tell Peter they thought they were being haunted by a picture?

'Well…' she began.

'We noticed the teeth marks on it, and, er, guessed it must belong to the dog…' Sam continued lamely.

Peter didn't look convinced.

'Where's Goldie now?' Abbie asked, hoping to change the subject.

'She's dead,' said Peter. 'She was fourteen, a good age. She never quite got over losing Mum, poor thing.'

Abbie felt a shiver run down her spine 'When did she die?'

'Just last Thursday,' he said. 'Ten days ago.'

'That's when it all began,' Abbie said to Sam. 'That was the first time I found Benjy's food bowl outside. And the first day he refused to go past the woodpile.'

Sam stared at her. 'You don't mean…'

'Yes, I do.' She turned to look at Peter. 'Mr McKenzie, I think Goldie came back to our house to find her photo.'

They told him the full story. He looked at them in disbelief at first, but then picked up the photo and ran his fingers over Goldie.

'Oh, you crazy girl. You missed your Mum so much, just like I do. Well, we'll have to put that right now, won't we?'

He stood up, and asked Abbie and Sam to follow him. At the end of his garden, under a gnarled old crab-apple tree, was a newly dug mound with a simple wooden marker.

'I buried Goldie there,' he told them. 'And now I think we should bury the photo with her. Then perhaps she'll be able to rest in peace, and give you and your poor dog some peace as well.'

Abbie and Sam stood silently, their heads bowed, while Peter knelt and scraped back some soil from the top of the mound. He carefully placed the photo face down, and covered it again. It might have been her imagination, but Abbie thought she heard a faint, but unmistakably grateful, little woof.

'Thanks, Peter,' she said. 'I think you're right.'

The End

What's Up with Benjy – Discussion

It's a Type 1 story, isn't it? Goldie's ghost wants that old photo of her mistress, which she always slept with, so she can sleep in peace again. All a bit unlikely, but then, so are most ghost stories, so don't let that stop you. As long as you are consistent regarding your rules for ghosts within the story.

In this one, the humans didn't sense the ghost but poor Benjy did (and I picture him lying with his head as low as possible, ears draped across the floor, paws over his eyes, poor love). The ghost can move physical objects. Goldie-ghost even knocked over a wheelie bin.

When I first opened up the Word document containing this story so I could copy it into this book, and read it through, I noticed I had Abbie suggest it could have been a possum that pushed over the bin in the night. A *possum*? In *England*? I must have tried to re-sell this story to one of the Australian magazines (it was originally published in the UK in *Take A Break's Fiction Feast*) and had left it Australianified (if that's a word. Spell-check says no.) I quickly switched possum back to fox. Any mention of a possum would pull most readers of this book straight out of the story, and leave them frowning and scratching their heads.

It's much easier writing for your home markets. Easier to get hold of them to study the type of story they take, and far, *far* easier to get the tone and language right. But if you are trying to sell a story abroad, do try to get your facts right.

Don't write about sizzling hot August days or snow at Christmas for the down-under markets. Do check details – in *What's Up with Benjy* Goldie is buried under a crab-apple tree. Common enough in English gardens but do they even have them in Australia?

Remember, Wikipedia is your friend. If in doubt, look it up.

Same goes for historical details, or stories intended for home markets but set abroad. Research is so easy these days with the internet at your fingertips – there's no excuse for getting something wrong.

Make up your ghost, but do put it in the real world, so the story is believable. Ghost stories require readers to suspend their disbelief in ghosts, for the duration of the story. Readers can only suspend one disbelief at a time, so everything else in the story has to be completely real. For that reason, I wouldn't attempt to mix aliens with ghosts, or add in a bit of sci-fi. Mind you, the womags tend not to publish many sci-fi stories, even though they seem to love ghost stories. I suppose alien stories don't give us that comforting 'there is life after death after all' feeling.

Think outside the box

Having said no sci-fi for womags, there is one exception. I've seen plenty of time-slip stories in womags – by this I mean stories where characters slip through time and appear in a different time period for a while before going back. That's basically time travel, which is sci-fi, isn't it? Ghost stories are a kind of time-slip story, as your ghost might well be from a different time period, with thoughts and values from the time in which they lived (think back to the very first story in this book, *We'll Meet Again*, as an example).

When deciding who your ghost is, think outside the box. I'm not going to say any more now, but with the idea of time-slip in mind, read this next story.

Safe As Houses

Shelley discovered the door while stripping the wallpaper from her dining room. The architrave had been removed, and the door had been wallpapered over.

'What on earth?' Shelley exclaimed. 'Mike, come and take a look at this!'

'Wow,' said Mike, putting down his scraper. 'That must lead directly into the living room. Wonder why it was blocked off?'

'I don't know,' said Shelley. 'Wish it wasn't, though. It'd be handy to have a door there, rather than having to go via the hallway.'

'Well, we could unblock it,' said Mike. He put his arm around Shelley's shoulders. 'We could put it back how it used to be. Do a bit of restoration work. This old cottage deserves it, don't you think?'

'Yes, definitely.' Shelley smiled at Mike. She loved the way he shared her ideas for the cottage – remove all its ugly seventies and eighties alterations, and decorate it in a style more appropriate to its age.

'I'll go and get some tools so we can get it open,' Mike said.

'We've no furniture against that wall in the living room. It'll mean bursting through the wallpaper on that side, but we'd planned to remove it anyway, hadn't we?'

'And we might as well start now!' Shelley said, laughing.

While Mike went to fetch the tools Shelley continued scraping off the wallpaper. They'd bought this cottage just a month before, and it was their dream home. It was situated on the edge of a pretty village, and although it clearly needed a lot of work they'd been able to see its potential straight away. Built of stone, with mullioned windows and an original heavy oak door, it felt solid and safe.

It had once been a rectory, so Shelley was told by Mrs Parkinson, who ran the village post-office. Shelley had popped in the previous week to pay her car tax and ended up sipping tea in the back room while Mrs Parkinson regaled her with tales of village life.

'Lovely to have a young couple living in the old rectory,' she'd said. 'And I'm delighted you're going to do it up.'

'Yes,' Shelley said. 'It's hard work, but it'll be worth it.'

'It will. Ooh, did I tell you I once saw ghosts there?'

'No?' Shelley had wondered whether the cottage was haunted – it was certainly old enough.

'It was when I was about five,' said Mrs Parkinson. 'I'd been taken there by my mother for tea with the vicar. I remember sitting in my best frock on the sofa in the living room, drinking a glass of milk and nibbling on a rock bun, oh so politely. Then suddenly two figures walked in through the wall. I spoke to them, but the adults couldn't see or hear them. They say children are more receptive to the spirits than adults, don't they?'

Shelley nodded, fascinated.

'Anyway,' Mrs Parkinson continued, 'something frightened them. They clutched hold of each other, then they just left – through the door to the hall, where they vanished.'

'Weren't you scared?' Shelley asked.

'No, dear. That cottage is a safe house, haven't you felt that? It'll always protect anyone inside it, I really believe that.'

Shelley had told Mike what Mrs Parkinson had said, but he'd just laughed. He didn't believe in ghosts, or 'any of that nonsense', as he put it. Scraping the wallpaper off the old door, Shelley wondered whether opening it might free the ghosts. But she wasn't scared - she knew what Mrs Parkinson meant about this being a safe house. She felt it too.

Mike was back with the tool box. 'Shell, can you smell gas?'

'No,' she replied. 'Can you?'

'I could, when I was out by the shed. Must be something to do with those road-works out there. Looks like they've clocked off for lunch now. I'll mention it to them when they return, if I can still smell it then. Right, let's get this door back in action.'

Twenty minutes and a lot of tinkering later, they'd freed the door and could pull it open. But it wasn't papered on the other side as they'd expected.

As they went through to the living room they both gasped.

'It's different!'

'Where's our stuff? Oh!'

It was their room all right, but not their furniture. There were heavy old-fashioned sofas and stuffed armchairs around the room.

The floor was polished wood with a semi-circular rug in front of the fireplace. A tea trolley sat in the centre of the room, set with a teapot, some crockery and a plate of buns. A small child sat on the sofa, holding a glass of milk, a plate balanced on her lap. She stared straight at them.

'Hello,' she said. 'Would you like a cup of tea?'

'Er, no thank you,' Shelley replied. 'Who are you?'

'My name's Vera,' the child replied. 'It's my birthday soon. I'll be six.' She smiled proudly at them.

'How lovely,' said Shelley. She grasped hold of Mike's hand. He was trembling. 'Mike, do you think…'

At that moment a door opened – the door leading to the hallway – and three adults walked in; two women wearing floral print dresses, and a man dressed as a vicar.

'Um, excuse us, we're just…' Shelley began. But the adults sat down and began pouring tea and chatting amongst themselves.

The little girl looked at Shelley. 'That's funny. They can't see you.'

'Ssh, Vera,' scolded one of the women. 'Remember what I said about being seen but not heard.' Vera scowled and nibbled on her bun.

'What's going on?' said Mike, loudly. 'Who are these people? Where's our furniture? You – what are you doing in our house?' He stood right in front of the vicar, but to no effect. The man just continued talking politely with the women.

'The girl's right,' said Shelley. 'They can't see or hear us. Only she can.' She went over to the sofa and sat down next to the little girl. 'Vera, can you hear me? Don't get into trouble, just nod if you can.'

Vera gave a slight nod.

'Do you live here, Vera?'

The little girl shook her head. 'Visiting,' she whispered. 'The vicar lives here.'

'Oh yes, this house used to be a rectory. Remember, Mike, I told you what Mrs Parkinson from the Post Office told me…' Shelley felt her stomach lurch as she recalled what else Mrs Parkinson had told her.

'I think we should go,' she said.

But Vera widened her eyes in alarm and shook her head. 'Stay,' she mouthed.

Shelley was about to ask why, but before she had the chance to say anything there was a huge explosion, coming from somewhere outside. She and Mike clutched at each other, instinctively burying their faces in each other's shoulders.

When the noise died down, Shelley raised her head. Vera was looking at them in surprise. She hadn't moved, and neither had the other people. The room was unchanged.

'Wha – what was that?' Mike said, sounding terrified.

'I don't know – a bomb?' said Shelley. But why weren't the people reacting, why wasn't the room damaged?

'Did you hear a loud bang?' she asked Vera. The girl shook her head slightly.

'Mike, I think the explosion was in our own time,' Shelley said. 'We need to get out, before we get trapped.'

'Our own time? What do you mean? Let's just go, this is way too weird for me. Where's the door?'

They turned to look for the door where they'd come in, but there was nothing there – just a blank wall. Shelley patted the wall but it was solid. The only door was the one to the hallway. She grabbed Mike's hand and pulled him towards it.

'Bye Vera, and thanks. I think we'll meet again, one day,' she said, as they opened the door and staggered through.

On the other side was devastation. The explosion had torn through the house, shattering windows, bringing down ceilings and rupturing pipework. There was a choking veil of dust and smoke hanging in the air, but even so Shelley could recognise her own furnishings and the tattered remains of her curtains.

Some one was hacking down the front door with an axe. A fireman burst through.

'You're alive, thank goodness! Follow me, I'll get you out of here.' He bustled them outside, where they were wrapped in blankets and led to a waiting ambulance.

'What happened?' Mike asked the fireman.

'Gas explosion,' came the reply. 'You're very lucky to be alive. Look at those two rooms – if you'd been in either of those you'd be toast.'

Shelley glanced back at the house. The two front rooms - the living room and dining room - had suffered the worst of the explosion. Both were burning fiercely, as firemen trained their hoses through the shattered windows.

'Yet there's not a scratch on you,' the fireman continued. 'I've never seen anything like it.'

Half the village had turned out to see what was going on. Mrs Parkinson pushed through the crowd and caught hold of Shelley's arm.

'I heard the bang this time,' she said. 'I told you it was a safe house. I knew it would protect you.'

Shelley didn't answer. She just stood looking with dismay at her ruined house.

Mike came over and put his arm around her. 'It looks bad, love, but it's nothing that can't be repaired. There'll be insurance money. And I think we owe it to the house, don't we, after what it's done for us?'

Shelley smiled at him. 'We certainly do. Thanks, house.'

The End

Safe As Houses – Discussion

This was one of those wonderful stories which arrived in my head fully formed, one Sunday morning as I lay snoozing in bed. Rather than leap up and write it immediately, I lay still and let the whole thing play out in my head. Later that day I went for a walk with my family and told them the plot, which helped firm it up. In the evening I sat down and wrote it, more or less as it is here. It was published by the first magazine I sent it to, and you can probably guess which one that was. Yes – it appeared in *Take A Break's Fiction Feast* in 2008.

It's an unusual ghost story because the 'ghosts' in it aren't actually dead. Little Vera Parkinson thought she saw ghosts in the house, and believed they were ghosts for most of her life – after all, they walked in through the wall, didn't they? That's exactly what ghosts are supposed to do! I loved using that clichéd idea of ghosts walking through walls in this way.

Is this a Type 1, 2 or 3 ghost story? It's not any of them. It doesn't fit any of my definitions. We don't have a ghost with a problem, no one is coming to terms with anything, and there's definitely no alternative rational explanation. I suppose it isn't really a ghost story. It's a time-slip story. But I included it here because it's a good example of how an apparent ghostly experience (Vera's, as a child) could have an entirely different (but still supernatural) explanation. In this story, the house itself has a kind of consciousness, which exists outside of time. It knows the explosion is imminent, so it sends them back in time to keep them safe.

I was talking earlier about suspension of disbelief. In the beginning of *Safe As Houses* the reader prepares to suspend disbelief about ghosts when Mrs Parkinson tells Shelley she once saw ghosts in the old rectory. So we start getting ready for Shelley and Mike to encounter the ghosts. There's a mid-point twist when we realise Shelley and Mike are in fact the 'ghosts', and that instead of suspending disbelief in ghosts, we need to suspend disbelief in time-travel. I think if I'd had actual ghosts as well as the time-slip idea, it'd all have got too complicated and unbelievable. One supernatural element is enough for any story, especially those of under 2000 words.

When looking through my back catalogue of ghost stories to include in this book, I came across an unpublished one in which the 'ghosts' are 'future echoes'. (I must have been watching a lot of episodes of the TV show *Red Dwarf* at the time.)

In my story a couple return to a hotel where they'd spent their honeymoon ten years earlier. They have a 'déjà vu' experience which reminds them of the ghostly experiences they'd had on their honeymoon. Subsequent events have them playing out exactly what the 'ghosts' they'd experienced ten years ago did, and they realise that on honeymoon they must have experienced an echo of their future selves.

This story was never published. Rediscovering it, I think it needs another layer adding. The best ghost stories (or other supernatural stories) are not just about the ghost. They need to be about the living characters as well. If you can take away the ghost element and still have a story worth telling, you've probably got a winner. My 'future echoes' story needs something more – perhaps the characters need to have issues which must be resolved, and this happens only when they realise that they are the ghosts they'd seen ten years ago. I haven't included that story in this book, because I might have a go at adding this extra layer, and see if I can sell it. If I do, I'll let you know via my womagwriter blog!

What are your rules?

Let's go back to proper ghost stories now. Ones with actual ghosts, not time-travellers or future echoes. Dead people.

I've mentioned several times that it's essential to decide on the rules for your ghosts. Let's expand on this a little more. You need to work this out before you start, and then be consistent throughout your story. Of course, you can have a completely different set of rules for each ghost story you write, and it is fun to try out different ideas. Here are a few things to think about:

1. Can your ghost move physical objects? Don't have your ghost walk through walls and yet also be able to throw things around, poltergeist-style. They can either handle physical objects or pass through them, not both. A poltergeist (and Goldie, in *What's Up With Benjy*, can be classified as one of these) should be able to be trapped in a room. Joan, in *We'll Meet Again*, can't move objects which is why she needs to possess Kelly's body. What about Harold, in *Still Here*? Well, he seems to be stuck on the sofa but when push comes to shove he can use the phone. (Or can he? Remember this was a Type 3 story with an alternative rational explanation.) The worst example of inconsistency in this rule I came across was in a story where a ghost's hand passed through the door-handle, leaving it unable to get out of the room. Um, if its hand passed through the door-handle, then surely its entire body could pass through the door!

2. Can your ghost move through space? And if so, how? Does it walk, fly, or transport itself anywhere it wants by thought? Joan in *We'll Meet Again* couldn't fly off to France in search of Jack. She had to rely on going there by car with Kelly. I think if you give your ghost too many magical powers it makes things too easy. Make it work to get what it wants.

3. How do the living experience your ghost? Can they see it, hear it, feel it? Don't forget the other senses of smell and taste. Or are they experienced only by a mysterious sixth sense? I remember reading a ghost story where the ghostly presence was nothing more than a waft of lavender perfume (actually that was the story which won a competition where I was short-listed – see my next story in this book).

4. Who was your ghost when it was alive? This might colour its actions or the way it speaks, especially if it's a very old, historical ghost. The oldest ghost I ever put in an (unsold) story was from the Iron Age.

And of course don't forget to think about why your ghost is haunting the MC now, what its problem is, and what needs to happen for it to be laid to rest. As with the living characters in your story, you need to know and understand your ghost well before you can write about it. Alternatively just start writing, and you may find the ghost starts to take shape, if that's not too spooky a metaphor. Once you've got something on paper you can always go back and edit it later to make it consistent, if you changed your mind about the rules half way through.

By the way, I've gone on about rules, but none of them are actually *rules,* you understand? I don't believe in laying down any laws for writers. This last lot should be your *own* set of rules for each ghost in each story you write, which will help you come up with a story that works. You decide them, you set them, and then break them if it works for your story. In fiction there are no rules, only words. (Plus the odd bit of punctuation and grammar, of course.)

Right then, let's have a look at another story. This one has not been published before, but was short-listed in *Writing Magazine's* annual ghost story competition way back in 2004. I've included it because it's a nice example of a story using a set of rules for ghosts which are different to the norm.

Home Haunting

I woke up on New Year's Day 2001 with the mother of all hangovers. The previous night I'd been at a farewell party for my beloved brother, Jason. He was off to New York to take up some high-flying job in finance. Boy, was I going to miss him. He'd always looked out for me, his kid sister. Even now I was in my thirties Jason was still my protector, the one I could always depend on. We had sunk a good few bottles of wine together, and now I was feeling the after-effects.

I groaned and turned over, pulling the duvet over my head. Some one was telling me to wake up, wake up, over and over again. At first I thought I was dreaming, but then I opened my eyes and winced at the first stabs of the headache which was to stay with me all day. You don't dream pain like that. And the voice was still there. It was the voice of a woman, elderly but still firm and strong. I heard it in my head, not through my ears; it's hard to explain but the voice was definitely inside rather than outside.

I looked around, trying to focus, wondering just how many bottles of wine Jason and I had drunk the night before. And there, in the corner by my wardrobe I saw it.

The curtains were still drawn, and it was a dull day, so it was fairly dark despite it being mid-morning. But just by my wardrobe door there was a pale shimmering, like the heat haze you see on tarmac roads on a hot summers day. As I stared, it seemed to take shape – human shape.

I clutched my duvet close around my neck and sank back to my pillow. 'Good grief,' I thought. 'I must have really overdone it.' I made a mental New Year's Resolution to cut out alcohol for at least a month.

'Oh, don't go back to sleep. I've been sitting here for hours waiting for you to wake up. Have you any idea how much you snore after you've been drinking?' It was the same voice, sounding loud and clear in my head. She sounded a little like my mother.

I sat up again and looked over to the wardrobe. The luminous figure was still there.

'Who… what…?' I stuttered. I wasn't scared; I think I was too tired and hung over to feel fear.

'Who am I, you mean. Or what am I? What do you think I am?' came the voice, with a gentle mocking tone.

I stared, trying to make sense of the hazy form, trying to decide if it and the voice were connected. If I was seeing things *and* hearing things then I was definitely in trouble.

'Well, are you going to answer or are you just going to keep staring straight through me?' She was openly laughing at me now.

'Are you a…um… sort of a…?' How could I ask if she was a ghost? If the voice didn't belong to a ghost she'd certainly think I was mad. Even if it did, perhaps calling her a ghost was considered rude in the spirit world.

'A ghost?' She finished the sentence for me. 'Yes of course I am. You knew that as soon as I started trying to wake you up. Come on, it's eleven o'clock, I've been waiting ages to talk to you.'

'Talk to me?'

'Yes, I'm bored, stuck here in this corner. I should never have moved the bed.'

'Moved the bed?'

'Will you please stop repeating everything I say? It's very annoying. Oh I suppose I need to explain it all again. I always forget I need to do that.'

'Explain again?' I was floundering, trying to get a grip on events but failing. 'You haven't explained anything yet.'

'Not this time I haven't, no. OK then, here goes. As you rightly guessed, I'm a ghost. What people don't know about ghosts is that we can't move. We stay where we died. In my case, that's right here, in this corner of this room. For the last couple of months of my life I was bedridden, I had the bed moved over here so I could get a better view out of the window.'

'So you lived here, in this house?' That gave me the shivers, to think someone had died, here, in my bedroom. 'If you don't mind my asking, when did you die?' I had to admit I was curious.

'In 2058. I was eighty-eight years old.' There was a hint of pride at her advanced years in her voice.

'But, 2058, that's…'

'In your future. Yes. Ghosts can travel through time, but not through space. I can go to any point in history, my history, but I can only be in this one place. Oh I do wish I hadn't moved the bed. I'd be so much more comfortable if I wasn't half in and half out of this horrid wardrobe.'

'I could move the wardrobe, if – are you planning on staying?'

'Yes, I'll stay a while, I think. Moving the wardrobe would be lovely. Perhaps you could put a chair here – that big red one you have downstairs in the sitting room would do nicely.'

And that's how I began to share my room with a ghost from the future. I shifted the wardrobe and moved the chair she'd asked for upstairs. I never asked how she knew I had that chair. I guess I assumed ghosts could see through walls and floors even if they couldn't float through them.

Over the next few months we had lots of long conversations, mostly in the evenings after I'd retired to my room. I was not a 'morning' person, so I was glad that my ghost never seemed to want to talk too much in the mornings either, when I was rushing to get ready for work. If the truth be told, I was quite glad of the company, now that Jason was living so far away. There I was, thirty years old, living on my own in a house I'd renovated myself. It was a lovely house, light and airy, with large gardens. I always dreamed I'd stay there for ever.

What did we talk about, my ghost and I? Well, we discussed current affairs, art, music, films. She had very similar tastes to me, and having lived through the same era as me she'd seen many of the films I had. It amused me when she referred to a film I'd just seen, one which had been released only the previous week, as a 'classic'. She was usually so careful not to tell me anything about the future. She didn't want to 'spoil things' she said.

We also talked about me. I found I could tell her anything and everything.

She understood how much I missed my brother Jason. I could confide in her, tell her my dreams and hopes, my excitement when the new chap at work asked me out, my disappointment when the date fell flat. She gave me advice too, on my love-life (or lack of one), on handling a difficult situation at work, on whether to buy a dog or not, on what to do about the overgrown trees in the garden. I didn't always take her advice, but when I did things seemed to go well so I began to trust her more and more.

She never told me much about herself. I asked her sometimes, had she married, did she have children, how did she die. But she was always evasive, and always managed to turn the subject back to me. She seemed to know me better than I knew myself.

One evening in the second week of September I went upstairs to change out of my work clothes as usual. The ghost was in the chair, but there was an odd atmosphere in the room. I knew she was unhappy, even before she spoke to me.

'I'll miss you,' she said. 'I've enjoyed this year.'

'What? Are you leaving?' I flopped down on my bed as was my habit when we talked. 'How can you leave, I thought you couldn't move from the corner?'

'I can move through time, remember.' There was a hint of impatience in her voice.

'But why are you going?' I was confused, we got on so well together. I wondered briefly if she thought she was cramping my style. It was true I made less effort to go out and meet friends, now I had someone at home to talk to.

' Because… well, it's kind of hard to explain. Put it this way, I don't want to er, live through the end of 2001 again.' She was being evasive again, as she always was when there was any mention of the future.

'Why? What happens?' I decided to push her this time. If she was really leaving I'd like to know why.

'Oh, I can't say, you know that. But it's bad. You'll need to be strong. There, that's all I can say.' She broke off with a sniff. She was actually crying.

'Bad? What kind of bad?'

'You wouldn't believe me if I told you. Anyway, as I said, it's time for me to go now.' She sighed.

'Where are you going?' I knew I'd miss her company.

'Oh, I think I'll try 2000 next. I might meet m... your brother.'

'You never told me whose ghost you are?' One last question.

'Whose ghost do you think I am?' She was smiling through her tears, I could tell. But she wasn't going to answer me directly, and perhaps I didn't really want to know.

We said goodbye, then she left. The chair looked solid again, the shimmering figure was gone, her voice sounded no more in my head. The room's emptiness hit me, and I looked at the clock, automatically calculating the time in New York. It was too early to phone Jason, he'd still be at work, up there in his office on the 60th floor. Instead I sat down to write my diary. *September 10th 2001. My ghost has left. Something bad is going to happen, and I'll need to be strong. Wish Jason was here.*

The End

Home Haunting – Discussion

Not a womag story – it doesn't follow the comedy story arc and have a happy ending. It's not a Type 1, 2 or 3 story. We leave the poor unnamed woman on the eve of 9/11. The reader, like the ghost, knows what's going to happen next, but the MC doesn't. (By the way, don't you just hate it when the MC in a story never gets a name? I do. But in this story I couldn't name her, because then I'd have had to name the ghost as well.)

So in this story I really played around with a different set of rules for the ghost. She can move through time but not through space at all. She's stuck in the exact spot where she died. But she can visit different years, chat to her earlier self, and presumably, if she goes back before her time in the house, she can chat to other occupants. When I first wrote a version of this story, I posted it on the old BBC *Get Writing* website. I remember one person criticising it with the comment that 'everyone knows ghosts can move and walk through walls'. Oh yeah? I thought. My story, my ghost, my rules. But I guess if you make your rules too wacky you might alienate some readers. Keep those ones for competitions, perhaps. I had a lovely letter telling me this one had been short-listed – praising the unusual ideas and the 'topicality' (this was in 2004, remember, when the events of 9/11 were still raw in people's minds).

If you can be original and use ideas that the competition judge or fiction editor hasn't seen before, your story will definitely stand a better chance of doing well.

They say there are only seven different basic plots (or five, or eight, or four, or thirty-six depending on which analysis of story-telling you read) so you're unlikely to come up with a completely different one. It'll be a 'coming to terms' or a quest, or a romance, or a 'rebirth', etc. But *how* you tell the story is up to you. Characters, setting, sequence of events, are all up for grabs. And when writing ghost stories, you have that *extra* element – use your ghosts, make up rules for them to suit the story you want to tell. You can also mix genres – have ghosts on a quest, ghosts being reborn, ghosts coming to terms. There is endless scope.

The MC and ghost in *Home Haunting* could easily feature in a sequel, in which both have to come to terms with the loss of Jason, buried in the rubble at Ground Zero. It would be a Type 1 story for the ghost and a Type 2 for the MC – an interesting mix! Or what about writing about a ghost coming to terms with its *own* death? Perhaps one in which the ghost doesn't even realise it is a ghost? (Have you seen the film *Sixth Sense*?) Or the opposite: I once wrote a story in which the MC thinks she is a ghost, and is apparently doing ghostly things. 'So this is what it's like being dead,' she thinks, as she floats above the rooftops and drops in on her grieving family who can't see her. She's just getting used to the whole set-up when strange voices sound in her head, bright lights shine in her eyes, and she wakes up from a coma.

The Ones Which Didn't Sell

I'm being very brave here. I'm going to include a couple of stories which I never managed to sell. They're not *bad* stories – I wouldn't dare inflict my really rubbish ones on you, dear reader! They're stories I felt were good enough to submit, but which were declined by the magazine editors. With the benefit of a few more years experience I think I know why, and I've included my thoughts after each story.

But what do you think? Would you have bought them? Let's play at being magazine editors. Put your critical head on and decide why the next two stories weren't good enough to publish.

Follow Me

'Who is she?' Ali asked her brother Mark, as they trudged past a statue of a skier situated in the centre of the Austrian ski resort.

'Don't know,' said Mark. 'Some female ski guide from the fifties, I think.' He gestured to a plaque fixed to the base. 'Died in 1962 in an avalanche after helping a party get down off the mountain in a storm, apparently.'

Ali gazed at the statue's face. She seemed to be looking longingly up at the mountain. 'Brave woman,' she said, as they crossed the street to the base of the ski lift.

Hoisting their skis onto their shoulders they went through the barriers, swiping their lift passes. Ali was glad there was no queue – the weather wasn't great and most skiers had decided to call it a day at lunch time.

They deposited their skis into the slots on the outside of the gondola, and sat down in the little cabin with relief. It was hard work trudging around in heavy ski boots.

'Right then, sis,' said Mark. 'Last run of the holiday, eh? The plan is to go to the top, then we'll ski down the blue run – the intermediate. There's a difficult black as well, but I don't suppose…?'

Ali shook her head. 'You're right – I'm not even

going to consider doing the black run. You know I don't like the steeper slopes. The blue will be fine.'

'You should push yourself a bit more, Ali. You'll never improve if you just stick to the easy stuff. If you followed me down you'd be fine. You might even learn something.'

Ali ignored him. He knew she hated following anyone. She always preferred to make her own tracks. Not only in skiing, but also in life in general. One thing was certain – you could never accuse her of being a sheep and simply following the herd.

She turned to look out of the gondola's window, back down at the valley which was now far below them. 'It's getting misty.'

'Hmm, yes. We're not going to be able to see too much on this run,' said Mark. 'It's going to be windy at the top, too.' The gondola was beginning to bounce and sway alarmingly on its cable. 'They'll close the lift if this gets any worse.'

Ali gasped. 'Not while we're on it, I hope!'

Mark grinned. 'Don't be daft, sis. They know which numbered cars are occupied. They wouldn't close the lift until the last occupied one has reached the top.' He sighed. 'Looks like this will definitely be the last run for us this holiday.'

Ali didn't answer. She'd just about had enough of skiing this week. Her thigh muscles were burning, her shins were sore where the boots pressed hard, and there was a bruise on her hip from a fall she'd had on the first day. She enjoyed skiing, but it had to be said, it was a tough sport.

At last the gondola lurched its way into the top station. As the doors opened, Ali wearily climbed out and retrieved her skis. Mark was already outside, clipping his boots into his skis and adjusting his ski goggles.

'It's windy all right,' he shouted over the roar of the gale. 'The blue run goes down this way. Come on, it'll be a bit more sheltered once we get off the summit.'

She shivered as she zipped up the neck of her ski jacket and tugged her hat down over her ears as tightly as she could. She wasn't just a fair-weather skier – a bit of wind and snow didn't bother her normally – but this was pretty extreme. She snapped her boots into her skis, looped the straps of her poles around her wrists and pushed off ahead of Mark in the direction he'd pointed.

They skied a short way to where a sign post marked the turn off for the two runs, black to the left and blue to the right. A row of poles planted in the snow and strung across with orange tape, flapping wildly in the wind, cordoned off the start of the blue run. There was a sign attached warning of avalanche danger.

'Blue run's closed,' said Mark. 'We'll have to do the black after all.'

'No!' Ali gasped. 'I can't, Mark.' She peered over the edge of the black run. It looked far too steep. 'How come the black's open if the blue's closed?'

'The blue loops round the mountain underneath a slope prone to avalanche. The black goes straight down. I guess that's why. Come on, Ali. It'll be ok once you get going.' He started pushing himself slowly towards the start of the black run.

'No!' she said again. 'Can't we go down in the gondola?'

Mark looked up the slope at the gondola station. 'I'm not walking back up there,' he said. 'Easier to ski down than climb back up. Follow me, for once!' He allowed his skis to slip sideways a little way down the slope. A couple of other skiers, their heads down against the wind, swooshed past them from the gondola and disappeared down the black run.

Ali was frozen with fear. The conditions were getting worse – the wind had picked up again and snow was blowing horizontally, stinging her face. She pulled her muffler up over her mouth and cheeks, and tried to tuck it under her goggles. Not easy with thick ski gloves on, but she needed to cover all exposed skin.

Mark had side-slipped a bit further down the mountain. She could only see his top half now; his lower half was hidden by the slope. He waved a ski pole at her and shouted something, but his words were carried away by the wind.

'I'm not skiing down there behind him,' she muttered. 'I'd rather go my own way.' She pointed with her ski pole at the gondola station, then bent to unclip her skis. As she hoisted them onto her shoulders Mark waved again at her. He pointed to himself then down the mountain, then to her and to the gondola. She nodded – yes, they'd split up. He could ski down alone while she took the lift. They would meet up at the bottom. She watched as he waved one more time, turned, and began to ski down. He was out of sight in seconds, swallowed up by the storm.

Ali began to trudge back up the mountain towards the gondola station. It wasn't far away, but walking was so much slower than skiing, and she was head into the wind now. She had to kick into the snow with every step, while the skis dug into her shoulders. It took fifteen minutes to get back up to the gondola station. Only one skier passed her in that time – a man dressed in the black and yellow outfit worn by the ski resort employees. He waved at her and shouted something as he passed, but she could not hear what he said, and just waved back.

Finally she reached the station and gratefully stepped inside, out of the wind. But the lift was not running. No gondolas were moving. A chain was across the entrance barrier, and the little control cabin was deserted. A sign informed her, as if she hadn't guessed, that the gondola was closed due to high winds.

Ali felt tears prick at her eyes. The lift was shut, the easy blue run was closed, and Mark would be half way down the mountain by now. She was alone in appalling conditions on the top of a mountain, with no way down but a black ski run which she was too scared to attempt. She considered waiting for the lift to reopen, but on checking her watch she realised there was only another hour of daylight left. They would not reopen the lift today even if the wind did die down.

There was no other option but to take the black run.

She took a deep breath, clipped on her skis and adjusted her goggles and muffler. 'Come on, Ali. You can do this. You *have* to!' she told herself, sternly. She pushed herself slowly away from the gondola station towards the signpost which marked the top of the black run.

The wind was even stronger than before, and Ali felt her muscles begin to lock up with fear.

At the top of the black run she paused, looking for Mark's tracks. But the blizzard had wiped out all trace of him. She was truly alone up here.

Stifling a sob, she edged her skis over the lip and cautiously side-slipped down a couple of metres. Goodness, it was even steeper than it had looked from above! She pushed herself forward and made a sharp turn. For a moment she felt out of control as her speed picked up. Terrified of falling on this steep slope, she pushed down hard with her heels and managed to bring herself to a shuddering stop, facing sideways across the slope, with her sticks planted firmly either side.

She panted heavily. 'I'll never get down this in one piece,' she muttered. 'If only I wasn't alone.' She looked back up the mountain, hoping someone might come but knowing that there was no one else above her, and now the lift was no longer running there was no chance of anyone else appearing.

For once, she wanted nothing more than to be a sheep and follow someone else.

Turning to face back down the mountain, Ali was surprised to see a faint figure few metres below her on the slope. The person hadn't been there a moment ago, she was sure of it.

'Hello! Can you help me?' she called. Her words were snatched away by the wind but the figure waved a ski pole at her, beckoning Ali to follow. Determined not to lose sight of her companion, Ali pushed herself forward and managed to make another turn; this time without losing control.

The other skier was nearer now, and Ali could see it was a woman, dressed in a red jacket and tightly fitting white ski trousers. She had a red bobble hat and odd double lens ski-goggles – they looked more like old aviator's goggles than ski goggles.

'Awful weather!' Ali shouted. 'Can we stay together down here?'

The woman nodded, and set off, making short, careful turns, zig-zagging down the slope in perfect control. Ali went after her, turning in the other woman's tracks. It was so much easier not having to decide for herself where to turn.

After a while the woman paused, and Ali slid gratefully to a stop beside her. The wind had lessened now that they were part way down.

Ali pulled down her muffler so she could speak more clearly. 'Thank you – this is really helping me. I was terrified up there!'

The woman smiled. She looked vaguely familiar. Ali wondered if she had seen her around the resort. 'I'm Ali,' she said. 'What's your name?'

'Liesl,' the woman replied. 'Shall we go on?'

'OK, I'm ready,' Ali said, and once again followed Liesl's tracks. The slope became less steep, and the going was easier. Soon they were below the tree line, and joined a wide gentle run which led right down to the village. Ali found herself speeding up on the last part of the run, making wide carving turns, still following in Liesl's tracks

There was a log cabin café at the bottom of the run; the lights in its windows looked warm and inviting. She swooshed to a halt in front of it, and looked around to thank Liesl again.

'Ali, thank goodness!' Mark appeared at the door of the café and trudged over to hug her. 'I heard the lift had closed and was so worried for you. I should never have left you. It must have been awful coming down alone.'

'I'm fine,' she said. 'I wasn't alone – a lady skied down with me. Did you see her – she was wearing a red jacket.' She looked around but could not see Liesl.

Mark frowned. 'You came down alone. There was no one else. I've been watching from the window of the café.'

'But I was following her all the way,' said Ali. 'She made it so much easier – I don't think I could have got down without her.'

Mark shook his head. 'You were definitely on your own, and you were the last person off the mountain. I was about to ask the café manager to call out the ski rescue service. Thank goodness that wasn't necessary.' He laughed. 'In any case, I can't believe *you* would actually *follow* anyone! That would be a first! Come on, let's get inside and I'll buy you a glühwein to warm you up.'

Ali shrugged and followed him inside. He was right – a glass of warm spiced wine was exactly what she needed. She sat at a table near the open fire while he queued at the bar. While she waited she gazed about her. The café was full of skiers who'd come down earlier, but there was no woman in a red ski jacket.

There were some old framed photos on the wall, of groups of skiers from the fifties and sixties. One photo showed a woman standing alone, looking up at the mountain. Ali read the caption beneath the photo. *Ski Guide Liesl Hermann, 1961.*

She smiled. Still guiding skiers down the mountain, fifty years after her death. Sometimes, following others who were more experienced than you was better than making your own way.

'Thanks Liesl,' she whispered. For a moment she thought she saw a glimpse of red at the corner of her eye, but when she looked round it had gone.

The End

Follow Me – Discussion

So, what do you think? It's an unusual setting: a ski resort in a storm, and with an unusual ghost: a ski guide. It has some moments of tension and drama as Ali finds herself stuck at the top of the mountain with the lift and easy blue run closed, and only the difficult steep run as a way down the mountain. She's in danger, and she's terrified, and there's no one about to help her, until the ghostly Liesl turns up.

I think the right elements are in place in the story, but it is missing layers. It's not enough for Ali to get herself in trouble and the ghost to turn up to save her.

As well as solving her immediate problem of being stuck in the storm, I think Ali needs to change in some other way. She needs to learn something new about herself, or resolve some other problem in her life (not related to skiing) as a result of this adventure.

You might have noticed I did try to do something like this – there are mentions that Ali never likes to follow anyone but always prefers to make her own path in life.

Skiing in Leisl's tracks makes her realise that sometimes following someone more experienced than you is better. But I didn't make enough of this.

The story would be improved if there was some back story showing Ali being pig-headed and refusing to follow someone's lead earlier, and perhaps boasting about not being one of the herd. The storm experience would then become a humbling one, making her realise there's no shame in letting someone else lead at times.

I recall I knew when writing this story that I'd need to add layers. But somehow I couldn't seem to get it right, and ended up with the rather half-hearted stuff about following. It ended up being a bit of a 'so what?' story. There's no real point to it – no universal truth, nothing to learn by reading it. And I sent it off to *Take A Break* anyway, knowing that it probably wasn't good enough.

It was duly rejected, and as is usual for *Take A Break*, no reasons were given. But I think its lack of depth is probably why. What do you think?

The other reason for its rejection would be that I wrote the story in January after returning from my own ski trip, and sent it off as soon as it was written. Given that magazines generally work three or more months ahead, the editor would have been looking for spring or Easter stories by that time. Had I held on to it, revisited it later in the summer and added the missing ingredients, then submitted it in the early autumn, I think it would have stood a much better chance.

Of course I could have done this anyway – despite being rejected once by *Take A Break* (the only real market for ghost stories), I could have reworked it extensively and resent it. The editor might have recognised it but would have given it another read through. And I might have sold it. But I'd fallen out of love with it, and so it was left languishing on my hard drive until I decided it was a suitable candidate for this section of my book.

OK, on to the second rejected story. Let's see what you think of this one.

I'll Wait For You

He walked softly through the moonlit woods, his footsteps making no noise on the frosted forest floor, his breath so quiet that even a fox, foraging for winter food, did not lift its head as he passed.

It was many years since he had been here, but he made his way with certainty, as though a path only he could see threaded its way through the trees to the shore of the little lake which lay hidden in the depths of the forest. The lake was iced over, glinting like diamond under the full moon. A gentle breeze ruffled the few remaining leaves clinging to the willows which clustered near the lakeside, and sent purple clouds scudding across the moon.

He trod carefully around the edge of the lake, making his way to the far side, heading for one particular tree. A large oak, solid and dependable, old as time and unchanged since his last visit. He sat down at its base, hugged by two buttress roots, leaned back on the gnarled bark and began to wait. Somewhere up above, he heard the hooting of an owl.

His thoughts returned to their first visit to this place. A summer day, almost a lifetime ago.

They had wandered hand in hand, talking and laughing and skipping through the sun-dappled woods, and gasping when they came upon the little lake, its surface rippled and dancing.

'Beautiful,' Rose had said. 'Simply beautiful. Oh Peter, can we stay here a while? '

He'd agreed, and they spread a picnic rug at the foot of the oak and sat down. Peter brought out ham and cucumber sandwiches, a flask of tea and a packet of custard creams from his rucksack. It felt like a feast. He'd known even then that he would never forget that simple meal.

Watching Rose dab at her mouth as she finished the last of the biscuits, Peter knew he was as happy as he could ever be, and that the woman sitting on the rug beside him was the only one he would ever love.

He took her hand, and raised it gently to his lips to kiss. When she giggled shyly and looked away, he cupped her chin in his palm and turned her face towards him.

'Rose,' he said, 'I have something to ask you. I love you and will love you for ever. Will you, my darling, spend the rest of your life with me?'

He watched, his breath held and his heart thumping, as her smile broadened and her eyes widened. 'Oh Peter, my love, of course I will!' She kissed him. 'If only we could stay like this for ever.'

He had taken her in his arms then, and they'd lain down together at the foot of the oak, melting into each other as the afternoon wore on and evening came.

They had come back every year for the first few years. Even after they married, this anniversary felt more special than that of their wedding.

Only when jobs took them to the other end of the country, and children made weekends away impossible, did they stop returning to this place.

Until now. Now, he was back, and soon, soon enough, she would join him here. He only had to wait.

Little by little, the moon traced its path across the sky. A badger came snuffling around the oak, but it wasn't startled by his presence. A wood mouse scuttled over his ankle. Before dawn, a blackbird sang in the oak's branches, and was soon joined by a cantata of birds, welcoming the new day.

Later, a group of boys came to play at the lakeside, throwing stones to try to break the ice. They didn't notice him sitting there, silently waiting.

Day turned to night, the night passed, the days passed and the seasons changed. Summer came, families picnicked by the lake, fathers skimmed stones across it and toddlers paddled in its shallows. Still he waited, unobserved.

Another winter came and went, until at last one bright spring day when the leaves glowed lime and the lake swarmed with tadpoles, she came. He heard her first, kicking up last year's dead leaves as she walked, humming a tune to herself. He saw her as she approached the lake side, and made her away around its edge, just as he had done. He stood to greet her.

When she saw him she smiled and held out her hands to him. 'I knew you'd be here,' she said.

'I waited for you,' he replied, taking her hands. How good it felt to touch her again!

'Thank you,' she said. She stood, gazing up at him, as beautiful to him as she had ever been.

'What was it, for you?' he asked, gently.

'Pneumonia.' She shook her head. 'But it only lasted two weeks, I barely felt a thing. Not like your cancer. That was a tough time.'

'I felt so bad, leaving you,' he said. 'And then not being there when it was your turn…'

'Hush, my darling,' she said, placing a finger on his lips. 'That's all over now. We can be at peace.'

'May I just ask you one thing first?' he said. 'I have loved you always. Will you, my darling, spend the rest of eternity with me?'

He watched as her smile broadened and her eyes widened. 'Oh my love,' she said. 'Of course I will! And shall we spend it here?'

He took her in his arms. They lay down amongst the roots of the oak, where they melted together into the lakeside earth as the day wore on, and the seasons wore on, and the years turned into centuries turned into millennia.

The End

I'll Wait For You – Discussion

What did you think? My husband quite liked this one when he read it. He thought it read well. 'It's as if you chose every word specially,' he said. Well, yes, that's generally what writers do. Bless him.

Reading it back now, I think it's a bit overly sentimental. I know I was trying for a lyrical, dreamy feel but I suspect it descends into slush here and there.

One magazine editor thought it was too guessable, with a well-worn theme. You, dear reader, would have instantly guessed the main character was a ghost, but that's because you're reading a book of ghost stories. If you weren't, at what point do you think you'd have realised what was going on? As for 'well-worn theme' – I have certainly seen other stories where the reason the ghost is hanging around is because it is waiting for a loved one to pass over. So yes, I suppose this has been done before.

The story is also a little raunchy, in a delicate kind of way. I hope you got that the foot of the oak was the place where they'd, ahem, shall we say sealed their love for each other. Sex before marriage, in the open air and in a womag – ooh er! That might have had something to do with why it was rejected. Perhaps I should have toned down the sentimentality and sent it to competitions instead. Never forget that womags aren't the only markets. If you've written one which doesn't feel right for the magazines, it's always worth trying a competition instead.

Ghostly love stories *can* work. Ghosts can fall in love with humans, humans with ghosts, or perhaps ghosts with each other. Which brings us to the last story in the book – and back to one which succeeded. It's a love story, but has a very different tone to the last one, and was published in *Take A Break's Fiction Feast* in 2012.

Letting Go

Five years I had the place to myself. Actually, if you add on the time before, it was nearer fifteen years. Just me in my own space. Everything was just fine.

Until *she* came. Emmeline, with her helmet hairdo and her pink nylon pinny. She changed everything.

I never owned the house. I just rented it, before. I paid the rent by standing order – hadn't seen the landlord for years. That was the way I liked it. I shopped online and had it delivered. I worked from home – actually I worked from this room. I did everything up here. My bed was against the wall there, my desk was under the window. My TV stood on a stand opposite the bed, with games consoles permanently attached to it. I hardly ever left this room.

They cleared the room within a week. I thought that was a bit disrespectful. But the landlord wanted to sell up. He redecorated the room – white with a beige carpet. I suppose the rest of the house was done up too, but I never went down to look.

When the family moved in with their teenage sons I thought they might use this attic room as a games room. It'd be a great place for video games and maybe even a snooker table. I was looking forward to watching the boys play.

But they just dumped a few boxes of outgrown toys and clutter in here, and left me alone again.

Until *she* came. Well, I suppose George came first. He's ninety if he's a day, as lined as an elephant's hide, grumpy as a camel, and snorts like a warthog in his sleep. The family moved their junk out and their Granddad in, all on one day. George didn't bother me much though. It was Emmeline, shackled to George like a prisoner in chains, who I objected to.

I materialised in front of her like a blast of arctic wind. George couldn't see me, of course, but Emmeline jumped out of her skin, or would have done, if she'd had one.

She recovered herself, pulled herself up to her full height with her feet at least five inches off the floor, looked up at me and demanded, 'Just who do you think you are?'

'I,' I said, 'am Stuart. This is my room.'

'No, it's *his* room,' she said, pointing to old George who was arranging his socks in a drawer. 'He can't cope on his own anymore, so he's come here.' She sniffed. 'Not that he was ever completely on his own. I've not left him for a minute. I've stayed true to my marriage vows. For better, for worse.' She rolled her eyes. 'Mostly for worse, forty-seven blinking years worse.'

'Well, you can't stay here. *I* haunt this room.' I waved my arms about to make the point.

'And *I* haunt *him*.' She folded her arms and fixed me with a look that could kill, if I wasn't already dead. 'So we're stuck here together. Hmph. Better get used to it.'

That was about a year ago. Emmeline's been dead seven years, she told me, and has hung around her husband like a noose around his neck ever since. She hates him, but she won't leave him.

At the beginning she nagged me endlessly about my appearance. I'd never bothered much with what I looked like, even before. I ignored her for months.

'Shave,' she ordered. 'And cut your hair!'

There was only one way to shut her up. I concentrated on projecting a new image – clean-shaven with a neat haircut. Shaved a few years off too, made myself about thirty.

'That's better,' she said, smiling slightly. 'But now your face doesn't match your clothes.'

I've worn the same grey jogging pants and Motorhead t-shirt since the day my appendix burst. I imagined myself into well-cut jeans and a checked shirt until they appeared.

Emmeline nodded her approval.

We became friends. Grudgingly to begin with, but gradually we warmed to each other. There was no choice really. As George spent most of his time in the room, so did Emmeline, and I never left it anyway.

One day I made a joke about her pink pinny. She sulked.

'Come on, Emmy,' I said. 'I changed, now it's your turn.'

I watched her morph from a dowdy old woman into a pretty young girl in a slinky green dress. Her hair was long and a startling shade of ginger. Her skin was porcelain white, and all her wrinkles and age spots were gone.

I hated to admit it, but I almost fancied her like this.

As time went on we became closer. When there's no one else you can talk to, it's only natural. One day she looked at George, snorting away on the bed during his daytime nap.

'I wonder if we could let go,' she said.

'What do you mean?'

'Let go. Leave here, leave him.'

'But we can't!'

'I think we could,' she said, 'if we tried. If we really wanted to.'

'Do you?'

She sighed. 'I've haunted him long enough. He doesn't even notice anyway – he just thinks the room's a bit draughty. Don't you want to go, too?'

'Well…'

'Come on. Let's try. Close your eyes. Think… upwards.'

I did. I imagined flying up, up, above the rooftops, into the atmosphere, feeling the wind on my face and the sun on my back.

I opened my eyes and the room was still there, with Emmy standing before me.

'Didn't work.'

'Try again,' she said. There was a sparkle in her eye as she took my hands and stepped closer. I closed my eyes again. I could feel her breath, and the warmth of her hands. I wondered what it would be like to hold her, to kiss her, perhaps…

And then I opened my eyes and we were in a meadow, full of poppies and butterflies and the sweet smell of freedom. Freedom from the room that had been my prison, in life and in death. Freedom from the grumpy, ungrateful old man who'd made Emmy's life a misery.

'Well, that worked,' I said. 'What were you thinking about?'

Emmy smiled. 'You.'

'Ditto,' I said, as I took her arm and led her across the meadow towards the rising sun and the next life.

The End

Letting Go – Discussion

Aw, though I say it myself, that one's so sweet! Ghosts as the main characters – the only real characters in the story as we never hear George speak or see him do anything. And there's some nice characterisation – Emmeline's helmet hair and pink pinny; Stuart the reclusive techno-nerd in his Motorhead t-shirt. A different set of rules are at work in this story – these ghosts can change their appearance at will, and eventually learn how to move to 'a better place'. And they do that using the power of love. What a nice message to end on.

Do ghosts really exist?

Except it's not the end. Not quite. I wanted to add a few words about true life experiences. It's impossible to read a book of ghost stories without considering your own spooky experiences.

I reckon if you put ten people together in a room, and ask them to tell you about their own real-life supernatural experiences (perhaps after a bottle or three of grown-up grape juice) at least half of them will have a story to tell. Some will tell classic tales of rustling skirts and creaking doors while staying in an old house.

Others will talk of things being moved in their homes while everyone swears blind they didn't touch the item. Or they'll recall visitations from loved ones who'd recently died. I heard of someone who found a bird inside her house, despite all doors and windows being firmly closed, each time a female relative died.

Do *I* believe in ghosts? I asked that question earlier in the book and promised I'd answer it later on. Now seems to be the time. The answer is a cagey yes and no. I'm a scientist at heart, and life's all about little electrical impulses in our cells, isn't it? Once the body dies the mind dies with it, and how can a mind or soul exist without a body? But there again, explain to me the time when I was a student, and my flat mate died in a tragic climbing accident. About five weeks later, he walked in through my bedroom door in the middle of the night. I woke up, stared hard towards the door which was partially open and *knew* that he was standing there. I even called out, 'hello?' And then he left.

Which doesn't quite answer the question, does it? I'm not sure whether or not I believe in ghosts. I *do* believe in ghost stories, however – their power to scare or amuse, or even comfort you.

Writing Prompts

I hope you're now itching to write a women's magazine ghost story! To help you get started, here are some ideas which you're welcome to use outright or use as prompts to trigger further ideas. Don't worry that everyone reading this book might write a story from the same prompt – even if they did you can guarantee that every story will be *completely* different. If you work better with deadlines, set yourself a kitchen timer for ten minutes, and see if you can come up with the start of a story using one or more of these prompts, in that time. If you don't like the stress of a deadline, then relax, close your eyes and let yourself daydream a story from one of these prompts.

Or just write the first thing which comes into your head related to the prompt, and then just carry on writing and see where it leads you.

If it goes nowhere, don't worry. Consider it a warm-up. Don't throw anything you've written away, ever. If you look at it again a month later, it just might spark some new ideas.

Five Senses

Write a story in which the ghost is only experienced using one of the five senses. Perhaps the 'ghost' is sensed only as a lingering smell of pipe tobacco? Or as the taste of cinnamon? Or as distant harp music, carried on the breeze?

Time-slip

Write a time-slip story, in which the main character doesn't just sense ghosts but is actually transported in time and affects events which subtly change things in her own time. OK, so not strictly a ghost story, but you could start out with her seeing a ghost, interacting with it and then finding herself in the ghost's time as a 'ghost' herself...

Seasonal Ghosts

Write a story in which a ghost appears only at a certain time of year or on a particular date. Christmas ghosts were probably done to death (groan, sorry) by Dickens but why not a Valentine's Day ghost, or a birthday ghost, or a Midsummer's Eve ghost?

Twist Endings

Write a story which the reader assumes is about a ghost, and at the end, reveal that the character is living.

How can you pull this off? Perhaps the character herself thinks she is dead, but is actually coming round from a coma. Or perhaps the character seems to be invisible to everyone around her, because she's one of those people everyone take for granted and never really notice. Until she does something out of the ordinary…

Write a story in which the main character is terrified of the ghosts in her house. They're everywhere but no one else seems to see them. Until finally they reveal to her that she's a ghost too… This would work better as a humorous story to avoid it being too dark.

Romance

Write a story in which your main character falls in love with a ghost from many centuries ago. She's a recluse who ignores the attentions of a living man, and enjoys the chivalry of her ghost. Until her living suitor finds a way of proving his worth…

Coming to Terms

There are endless variations of stories in which a ghost helps the main character come to terms with their loss. These stories can be very emotional. If you can bear to, mine your own memories of losing someone close. What experience might have comforted you and helped you move on?

(I would only advise writing stories based on your own loss years after the event. By all means write something soon after a death as a way of helping yourself come to terms, but don't try to sell those early pieces. They're too raw, and you might regret sharing something so personal. But with the perspective of time, those feelings can be used to flavour and colour a story.)

A character takes ownership of her late father's dog. She's not a dog lover, but when she takes the dog for a walk and it leads her to her father's favourite places, she gradually begins to get over his loss.

A character who was never any good at cooking, tries to make a special dinner for someone. She'd always phoned her mother for advice in the past, but her mother is now dead. But while cooking, somehow she can hear her mother's voice in her head, and she manages to produce a spectacular meal, and this helps her come to terms. Or use the same basic concept, and have a late father advise on DIY problems.

Ghostly Settings

Ghosts in creaky old houses are old hat. Why not have a ghost which haunts a soccer stadium? Or one which hangs around on a river bank, where courting couples come for summer picnics? Or one which lives backstage at the local amateur dramatics theatre? Or one which inhabits the stationery cupboard at the office?

What triggers your ghost to appear?

Write a story in which a particular event causes the ghost to appear. Pick something simple – perhaps lighting an open fire, cutting back a Clematis, moving an old piece of furniture to a different position. Every time the action happens, the ghost appears.

Location

Send your characters on holiday to experience the ghost. Not staying in the clichéd old converted castle, but in an all-inclusive Benidorm hotel. Or in a tent in the furthest corner of a campsite. Or in a poky room on the top floor of a run-down city hotel. Or in a theme park, where the ghost haunts the roller-coaster, or the hot-dog stall, or the children's Humpty-Dumpty display.

Who's your ghost?

Ghosts don't have to be from the past. Why not have one from the future – assume your ghosts can travel through time? Alternatively, have a ghost from the very distant past. Medieval, iron age, Roman – get out your history books and be inspired!

Ghosts don't have to be human – at least, they don't have to materialise as a human. I like the idea of a butterfly appearing whenever your bereaved main character thinks of her lost partner.

OK, that's your lot, I've run out of ideas for now. But it didn't take too long to write that set. Whether they're any good or not is up to you, and your imagination. If they did nothing for you, try spending an evening writing your own set of prompts which you can come back to later. Don't sit in a quiet room to do this – you need external stimulus when compiling ideas lists. If you've half an eye on the TV perhaps some news item or something a soap opera character says could turn into a story prompt. Maybe you can even guess (UK readers, anyway!) what was on TV while I was writing this section of the book?

And Finally

I hope this book has kept you entertained, and perhaps inspired you to write a ghost story of your own. If you do decide to write one, wait until late evening, when the rest of the household has gone to bed.

Turn your lights down low, perhaps write just by the glow of your computer screen. Or light a few candles, and write longhand in a notebook. Leave your curtains open, so that anyone or any *thing* could be looking in at you.

Put on some creepy music, or write in silence, listening to every creak and groan of your house. Sit with your back to the door.

Write *scared*.

If you sell a story inspired by reading this book, do let me know! I can be contacted via my website www.kathleenmcgurl.com or my 'womagwriter' blog www.womagwriter.blogspot.co.uk. I always love to hear from other writers.

Good luck and happy writing!

Further Reading

How to Write and Sell Short Stories by Della Galton – the queen of womag fiction takes you through the process from start to finish. Accent Press.

The Short Story Writer's Toolshed by Della Galton – a snappy no-nonsense guide to the art of writing stories. Soundhaven Publishing.

Monkeys with Typewriters by Scarlett Thomas – an in-depth look at the power of fiction and the structure of stories. Canongate Books.

Secrets and Rain by Cally Taylor – a collection of published and award-wining short stories which will warm your heart. KDP Publishing (ebook only)

Tears and Laughter and Happy Ever After – a collection of 26 short stories by various womag writers. Blot Publishing.

Diamonds and Pearls – another collection of women's magazine short stories, with a percentage of each sale going to a breast cancer charity. Accent Press.

Short Circuit: A Guide to the Art of the Short Story (ed Vanessa Gebbie) – a collection of essays about the art and craft of short story writing. Salt Publishing.

Back to Creative Writing School by Bridget Whelan – a superb book of inspiring writing exercises to get your creative juices flowing. KDP Publishing (ebook only)

Acknowledgements

My sincere thanks to Sally Quilford and Della Galton, who read and commented on the first edition of this book before I dipped my toes into the shark-infested self-publishing waters.

Thanks too to Della for being an ever-inspiring writing teacher.

And of course, thanks as always to the wonderful Write Women. Without you lovely lot I'd have given up writing years ago. The value of your friendship and support is immeasurable.

About the Author

Kathleen McGurl lives in Bournemouth with her husband and younger son, her elder son having flown the nest. She always wanted to write, and for many years was waiting until she had the time. Eventually she came to the bitter realisation no one would pay her for a year off work to write a book, so she sat down and started to write one anyway.

Since then she has sold dozens of short stories to women's magazines. These days she is concentrating on longer fiction, and is currently trying to find an agent for her full-length time-slip novel, while also writing another in the same genre.

She works full time in the IT industry and when she's not writing, she's often out running, slowly.

Short Stories and How to Write Them

by Kathleen McGurl

An anthology of women's magazine short fiction, plus notes on how to write your own.

Written in the author's friendly, chatty style, this book takes you through the components needed for a womag short story.

Available as a paperback or ebook from all Amazon websites.

11503089R00079

Printed in Great Britain
by Amazon.co.uk, Ltd.,
Marston Gate.